DARK DESIGN

Caroline Lane didn't mind being alone in her pleasant house — though she missed her husband when he was away on his frequent business trips — until the evening of the mysterious phone-call that introduced Neil Fuller into her life. With his coming came doubts that led her to question her husband's real whereabouts, even his identity. In pursuit of the truth, she discovered a dead man and his murderer and, ultimately, the answer to the problems that been troubling her.

FREDA HURT

DARK DESIGN

Complete and Unabridged

LINFORD
Leicester

First published in Great Britain in 1972

First Linford Edition
published 1997

Copyright © 1972 by Freda Hurt
All rights reserved

British Library CIP Data

Hurt, Freda
   Dark design.—Large print ed.—
Linford mystery library
   1. Detective and mystery stories
   2. Large type books
   I. Title
823.9'14 [F]

ISBN 0–7089–5066–3

Published by
F. A. Thorpe (Publishing) Ltd.
Anstey, Leicestershire
Set by Words & Graphics Ltd.
Anstey, Leicestershire
Printed and bound in Great Britain by
T. J. Press (Padstow) Ltd., Padstow, Cornwall

This book is printed on acid-free paper

1

THE sudden trilling of the telephone-bell sent a nervous thrill through the slim small boned body of Caroline Lane and widened her narrow hazel eyes. She was seated at the heavy Victorian desk in the small room she called her writing-room, facing the window that in daylight gave her a view of the sloping lawn and the willows fringing the stream that divided the garden from the meadow beyond, trees that gave her house its name of Willow Lodge.

It was a mild September evening and the sash window was open at the top, letting in an occasional moth and flying beetle as well as scents that mingled the lingering summer sweetness of stocks and tobacco plants with the first odours of decay. It was very quiet. The staccato sound of the typewriter, coming in brief bursts, had only emphasized the silence of the house, the stillness of the darkened countryside outside.

Caroline was used to being a good deal alone, and though, of course, she missed Gordon when he was away on one of these trips of his, there were pleasures to be found in solitude, such as long measures of time that could be devoted without interruption to the writing of one of the children's historical novels that brought her in quite a respectable income and provided active employment to an imagination that had expanded without much encouragement in her early youth. Telephone calls were not frequent enough to constitute a nuisance, but this one had jerked her back from a herdsman's hut in the thirteenth century.

She was tempted to let it go unanswered. But it might be her husband ringing from Newcastle, or even somebody trying to find out whether or not the house was occupied this evening. There had been burglaries recently in the neighbourhood and that was rather an alarming thought. Her small hand, that had been hesitating over the receiver, quickly descended and lifted it, cutting off the irritating trilling.

"Hallo," she said, in her quiet, low pitched voice. "Caroline Lane speaking."

There was silence. She felt alarm beginning to grow in her as she remembered that thought about burglars and half expected her caller to put down the phone without responding.

"Who is it? What do you want?" she asked.

"Good evening," said a masculine voice she did not recognize. "Is Mr. Lane there, please?"

"My husband?" said Caroline. "I'm afraid he's — " At the last minute she substituted 'very busy' for 'away'. For though the voice sounded quite pleasant in tone and suggested a man of some education, it occurred to her that it would be unwise to let a stranger know one was spending the night alone in a fairly isolated and vulnerable house. "Who is speaking, please?" she added.

There was another brief silence.

"My name wouldn't mean anything to you, I'm sure," replied her caller, after this pause. "But I would like to speak to your husband, in spite of his being — very busy. Would you tell him it could be important, please."

"I'm sorry. I couldn't do that without even knowing who was calling," Caroline said, feeling as if points were being scored in a curious kind of contest.

She listened to another silence, and was about to put the receiver down when the voice spoke again in her ear, abruptly, as if anticipating this intention.

"My name is Neil Fuller," it said. "*He* will know it."

She began to feel a little foolish and wondered how she could go back on her previous statement that her husband was merely busy, and then thought of a way.

"Hold on a moment, please, Mr. Fuller," she said politely, laid the receiver down upon the desk, pushed back her chair and walked to the door. There she stood for a few moments, smiling a little wryly at her own deviousness. Then she returned to the desk, picked up the phone, and said:

"I'm sorry. Gordon doesn't appear to be in now. He must have slipped out a little while ago."

"I see. Have you any idea where he has gone?"

Caroline hesitated. There was something about the tone of that 'I see' that almost suggested Mr. Fuller understood only too well. It made her uneasy again.

"Perhaps to the local pub," she said.

"The Hand in Hand? No. I don't think so. At least, he hasn't arrived here yet," said her caller.

"You're — you're phoning from the Hand in Hand?" she faltered.

"Yes, Mrs. Lane," answered Neil Fuller, and was silent again.

A conviction that she was being in some way got at angered and disturbed Caroline.

"I'm sorry I can't help you," she said abruptly, and put back the receiver.

But she found it hard to concentrate on her work again. Had it been her imagination that there had been something odd about that call? Suppose it had been all perfectly genuine and this Neil Fuller really did have important matters to discuss with Gordon. Had she done her wifely duty in cutting him off so sharply, without even asking if she could take a message? She was afraid Gordon wouldn't think so. Not that he would reproach her openly, but he might look at her with that strange cold expression that sometimes came into his light blue eyes, making her feel there was an icy gulf between them.

She wished suddenly that she knew more about her husband's business affairs. Ten months ago, when they had married, he had told her that he was a salesman for a firm of export agents, which meant that he would be away from home a good deal. She knew the name of the firm, and sometimes Gordon mentioned particular goods being handled, but naturally a man wanted to forget his work when he was relaxing at home. She might have been a little tactless at first, but she had not needed more than a hint from her new husband to grasp that. Even so, she had questioned occasionally his need to be off for a week or more at a time, chasing some consignment or other, but he had explained that his bosses liked the personal touch, rather than mere brief notes and phonecalls, and liked to make sure, by actual inspection, that their customers were getting what they asked for.

Perhaps, thought Caroline now, she should have told this Mr. Fuller to ring Dobson and Perks in the morning, though unless his business really was connected with them, old Dobson, as Gordon called him, might have some rude things to say. Apparently, he had a particular objection to mixing private affairs with business. From the beginning Gordon had warned her never, never to ring him at the office.

Caroline sat biting her lip and staring unseeingly at the sheet of paper in the typewriter. A large beetle blundered in and flew round the light, flicking the shade loudly with its wing-case, and she jumped up with an exclamation and drew the curtains across the window, wondering why she had not done this before, instead of sitting there on view to any prowler who might be around. Even with the curtains drawn the light would show and tell anybody who had taken the trouble to learn something about the household that she was alone here.

She went out into the hall and switched on the light there, illuminating a brass bowl full of dahlias that looked extraordinarily gaudy in the sober surroundings of dun coloured carpet, brown varnish and furniture of dark oak.

She really must do something about all this, she thought, glancing up the gloomy staircase where shadows seemed to lurk round the bend tonight. After all, the fact that Aunt Lilian had never wanted to change anything need not inhibit herself and Gordon. Only at first it had seemed so wonderful to be the owner of everything that the house and all in it had appeared to her well-nigh perfect. In a curious way she had not really seen it as it actually was, she decided. Just as, up to now, she had enjoyed an illusion of perfect safety during her spells of solitude here.

Now, she felt vulnerable.

In a slightly shamefaced way, she went to the front door and put up the chain, feeling glad that her godmother had been strong on the subject of bolts and bars when she had lived here with her elderly maid.

She switched on the lights in the big old fashioned kitchen, too. Colonel, the black and white cat with the luxuriant whiskers, whom she had inherited with the house, greeted her with a sleepy chirrup from his chair by the stove.

What she needed was a watchdog, she thought, stroking the cat's smooth head.

"You wouldn't mind, would you, puss?" she said aloud. "Not if we had it from a puppy and you could assert your superiority from the start."

She would speak to Gordon about it when he got back in two days time. About redecorating the house and buying new carpeting, too. She could afford it, though Gordon had a way of keeping a protective eye on the way she spent her quite hard earned money.

Caroline smiled down at the purring cat, and Colonel, as she withdrew her hand, flicked an ear, covered his eyes with a paw and went to sleep again with an air of quiet determination.

His mistress had gone to shoot the bolt on the backdoor. Then, reassured, she went back to her writing-room, leaving a blaze of lights behind her, and tried to settle down to work once more. But the spell was broken. She found herself unable to dismiss Mr. Fuller and his phone call from her mind.

Perhaps, she thought suddenly, it was not too late to do something about it. At least she knew where the call had been made from. Impulsively, she reached out a hand to the telephone.

Mimi Eccles answered from the Hand in Hand. Caroline recognized her rather asthmatic voice straight away.

"I had a call from your place about twenty-minutes ago, Mrs. Eccles," she said after a brief exchange of greetings. "A Mr. Fuller rang me."

"That must have been the red headed gentleman who left about ten minutes ago," said Mimi against a background of manly voices.

"What was he like?" blurted Caroline.

"Like?" Mrs. Eccles sounded puzzled. "Wasn't he a friend of yours, Mrs. Lane?"

"No," answered Caroline, adding quickly: "That is, he knows my husband. I've never met him. That's why I'm asking what he's like."

"Oh. Yes, Mrs. Lane. I see." But Mimi still sounded surprised.

"Well, as I said, he's got red hair," she told Caroline. "Very nice, really. Wasted on a man. You can say what you like, long hair don't seem right on the other sex, though I can't say I'm one to fancy beards, neither."

"Do you mean this Mr. Fuller has long hair and a beard?" asked Caroline, startled at the image this conjured up in her mind.

"Oh no, dear," answered Mimi. "Not like that at all. What you might call nicely groomed, in fact. Young, but not a boy. Mature, if you know what I mean, *and* knows how to talk to a lady, which some don't, I might tell you."

Caroline could imagine the plump

beringed hand touching the elaborately dressed blonde hair at this point, or smoothing one plump, tightly girdled hip.

"Had you seen him before?" she asked.

"Not to call to mind, Mrs. Lane," answered the landlady. "In fact, I thought to myself when he walked in, 'Hullo, you're new'. I served him myself, and then he asked did I know you and Mr. Lane."

"He mentioned us by name?" said Caroline.

"No, he didn't," answered Mrs. Eccles thoughtfully. "'The people at the house called Willow Lodge,' was what *he* said. And *I* said 'You mean Mr. and Mrs. Lane.' And I remember he said 'Mr. George Lane, that is, isn't it?' and I said 'Not George it isn't, because I've heard his wife call him Gordon.' That's right, isn't it Mrs. Lane?"

"Yes," said Caroline. "That's right."

"Then he said did I know if Mr.

Lane was at home, and I said I didn't for certain, though, I did know he'd gone off on one of his trips not so long ago. But old George Binwell, who has to know everything, chipped in that he knew Mr. Lane wasn't due back till Wednesday — had heard him say so in here the Saturday before last."

"And he telephoned *after* that?" said Caroline.

"Yes, Mrs. Lane. I had to serve somebody else, but I heard him ask old George to keep an eye on his beer while he went to the call-box outside and then he came back and finished his drink and left like I said."

"I see," said Caroline.

"Are you thinking he was just fishing for information about you and Mr. Lane, dear?" said Mimi, who was quite bright sometimes. "Because he *did* know your husband, at least by sight. When I said his name wasn't George he gave an ever so good description of Mr. Lane and said 'That's him, isn't it?' and of course

I had to say 'Yes it is.'"

Caroline, who had rung the Hand in Hand with the intention of asking to speak to Neil Fuller again if he was still there, was silent, thinking over her previous conversation with the man in the light of this new information.

"There's nothing wrong, is there, Mrs. Lane?" asked Mrs. Eccles, adding: "Look, I'm ever so sorry, but I've got to ring off. Larry can't cope on his own."

"Yes. It's all right, Mrs. Eccles. Nothing really to worry about," Caroline assured her. "Goodnight."

But she didn't feel as convinced as she tried to sound. In fact she still felt there had been something distinctly odd about that call. Only she didn't want Mimi Eccles speculating and talking about the matter, having some vague idea this might do harm to Gordon.

"But what has he been up to?" The question burst through into her conscious mind from somewhere deep down where it had been lurking, and with it came a truth she had been hiding from herself since her wedding day. The fact that she did not whole-heartedly trust her husband. As with her other surprise bonus, the house, she had been so delighted by the novelty of possession that she had never allowed herself to take a long hard look at Gordon. Even now, she did no more than glance before pulling back the veils and burying her doubts as deeply as she could — which was not so deep as before.

She did not attempt to go back to work, but wandered restlessly about the downstairs rooms, picking up a book and flicking over the pages before putting it down again, switching on the television in the small sitting-room and turning it off again after ten minutes viewing, going into the seldom used drawing-room and staring at a portrait of her godmother as a girl, painted by an Edwardian artist who had fallen into total obscurity.

The idea had occurred to her story-teller's mind that perhaps this man's reputation had rocketed mysteriously and the picture was now worth a fortune, that Neil Fuller had become aware of her ownership of it and was out to steal it. But after staring at Aunt Lilian's sentimentalized youthful representation for a few moments, she dismissed this notion as sheer fantasy. The artist had had just enough talent to bring out a hint of young Lilian's true character in the eyes, and it was plain that even then, her strong point had not been imagination. The painted gaze accused Caroline of having too much.

She longed now for company. But her one real friend in the neighbourhood, the local Librarian, Mary Green, was abroad on holiday. Her girlhood companions had all married and scattered, and Gordon had not encouraged the forming of new friendships. It was more fun being on their own, just the two of them, this first year of their married life, at least, he had maintained. The implication had been flattering to a naturally shy and reserved young woman and Caroline had agreed.

She was on her way to the kitchen again, determined to wake the cat up and carry him back to the sitting-room with her, when she thought she heard a car-door shut outside the house.

Surely not a caller! She glanced at her watch. It was past ten o'clock. She stood in the gloomy hall, listening. Was that a footstep? No. Yes. But when the doorbell shrilled it sent a thrill along her nerves as the phonebell had done earlier that evening.

Should she ignore the bell, hoping the late caller would go away? But she had been wishing for company. And it was plain to whoever was ringing that she was at home and up, by all the lights. What was she standing there for? It was ridiculous to be so nervous!

The bell rang again, startling her afresh, though she was expecting it. With relief she remembered the chain on the door. She would leave it up when she opened the door until she saw who was outside.

She switched on the porch light first, then opened the door as far as the chain would allow and looked round it, her delicately featured face, with its pale almost transparent skin, framed in her straight dark hair, appearing with a bodyless effect to the man waiting on the step.

He stared down at her from his considerable height in silence, the porch light making a fiery crest of his thick red hair.

2

FOR a long moment neither uttered a word. Then the stranger said: "Mrs. Lane?" in a tone that sounded faintly surprised, as if, she thought, she was not quite what he had expected.

He, too, was a little different from the image Caroline's mind had formed after Mrs. Eccles's description, but, in a way, more alarming. She had not pictured him so big, or with such a bold unblinking stare of tawny eyes under frowning brows.

She had answered automatically: "Yes," to his question. But immediately wished she had not.

"Look," she said quickly, "my husband isn't here, and it's late. I don't know what you want, but it's nothing to do with me, so will you please go away."

For a moment he continued to stare

down at her as if he hadn't heard. Then the frown relaxed and he gave the faintest of smiles.

"Goodnight," he said abruptly, and marched away down the drive to where the lights of his car pierced the darkness at the gate.

Caroline shut the door, astonished at the ease of her victory, and now, perversely, wishing she had not been quite so discouraging. What a coward she was! Of course the man was Neil Fuller. She had missed the opportunity of asking him what his business was with Gordon. Why had she said it had nothing to do with her? How could she know? He probably thought her a fool as well as a coward. That was why he had smiled in that manner.

Profoundly dissatisfied with her own conduct, she was puzzled and concerned by his. Why had he called, knowing that Gordon was away? For it was obvious he had not believed her story of a husband who had just gone out, understandably now she knew that he had been told that Gordon was away and would not be back till Wednesday. But perhaps he had just been making sure.

What *was* the important matter that had induced him to make that call in the first place?

Colonel asked to go out, and she unbolted the back door, forgetting her previous nervousness, and absently watched him stand cautiously surveying the darkness beyond the spilling light, before stepping gracefully over the threshold and becoming another small shadow in the night. She did not trouble to push the bolt home again. Rightly or wrongly, she no longer feared an intruder, and yet she had a deep sense of some threat hanging over her, a menace, to her peace of mind.

Suddenly she knew why she felt like this. She realized the meaning of the softening of Neil Fuller's expression before he had left. It had been compassion that had lowered his intense gaze and brought that little smile to his set lips. He had been sorry for her. Simply because of her silly fear of him? Or because he had knowledge of trouble as yet unknown to her — trouble for Gordon, and so affecting her?

Or was he, himself, bringing the trouble, and had he relented at sight of her? This could be, she decided, though she did not imagine that her charm had brought it about. Of course she was not beautiful or glamorous or exciting to men. Neil Fuller had probably found her just pathetic. Only Gordon had been attracted enough to break down the wall of shyness and reserve she had built around herself with his brief, ardent, determined courtship.

Whatever he had done, she should remember that.

Sitting at the kitchen table, resting her chin in her hands, she sat up abruptly, pulling her thoughts up, too. She told herself reproachfully that she had not a reason on earth to suppose that Gordon had done anything he shouldn't. She had no grounds for such a suspicion, except the odd behaviour of another man.

It was true, of course, that she had not actually known him very long, and had married him on remarkably short acquaintance. Just two months and three days after their first meeting, to be exact. It was also true that she had met no member of his family. But then, he had none. Like herself, he had been an only child of parents who were already middle-aged when he was born, so that they had both died when he was under thirty. The few friends he had seemed to have been recently made. But he had not lived in England for several years, he told her, and before that had shared a home with his parents in Norfolk, so naturally his old friends would be abroad, or living north of the Thames, not down here in Kent. Though one would have thought they would have come to London from time to time. And wasn't it rather odd that he never seemed to hear from them or talk about them?

She had not consciously considered these things before, but had just accepted them with Gordon, as she had accepted the old-fashioned furnishings of Willow Lodge. Even now, she had a feeling of disloyalty in deliberately questioning these circumstances that appeared to surround her husband like a mote round one of the Norman castles in her story. But could it be that Neil Fuller had the means of providing a bridge?

Her mind had come full circle and was back with the red headed man once more. She must stop all these speculations. They were worrying and unproductive and probably unnecessary, too. The phone call and the visit might easily have nothing to do with Gordon in reality. Neil Fuller might well have heard of him for the very first time when asking questions at the Hand in Hand, and then devised some confidence trick with herself as intended victim. Only she had foiled him by keeping the chain on the door and refusing to have anything to do with him.

Or he could have picked the name, Lane, out of a local telephone directory before calling at the public house, discovered there that her husband was away, and decided to pass himself off as an old friend of Gordon's. She would probably never see him again.

She got up from the table, deciding that the whole matter was over and done with, become simply something to talk over with Gordon when he came home on Wednesday. And yet — and yet she remained uneasy.

Colonel accompanied her up to bed that night, a privilege she was glad to allow him, but one he was never granted when her husband was at home. Their bedroom was definitely a place where two were company and three none, she told him, even when the third was only a eunoch of a cat.

He ignored the insult, stood on

her chest and kneaded the bedclothes enthusiastically, purring loudly and gazing into her face with a flattering softness in his yellow eyes. Then he curled up beside her on the eiderdown and let his songs gradually cease as he surrendered happily to sleep.

There was something very soothing about his simple affection and pleased acceptance of luxurious living, and, before she would have thought possible, Caroline, too, was overcome by slumber.

She woke from a confused dream of Aunt Lilian, who was not really dead, she thought, but had returned to make a new will, leaving Willow Lodge to Neil Fuller.

Colonel's uplifted voice roused her from this disturbing fantasy, as he stood at the door demanding to be let out. It was daylight, the eiderdown was on the floor, and the bedside clock had stopped at ten past four. She had forgotten to wind it.

Going downstairs in her long dressing-gown, she nearly fell over the cat who had stopped abruptly in his rapid descent ahead of her and was now glaring at the front door. Caroline herself froze into immobility, as, with a curious rattling sound, the door slowly opened to the extent of the chain, which she had left in place all night.

"Who's there?" she called, with a quaver in her voice.

"Me," answered a familiar voice, as Mrs. Hedges's broad pink face and curious eyes appeared in the opening, her grey brown hair wind-blown where it was not covered by her crocheted pudding basin of a hat.

"Oh, I'm sorry," cried Caroline, hurrying down to unfasten the chain and let in her daily help, while Colonel, after a slight pause in the hall to satisfy a brief curiosity, slipped out through the opening, avoiding the stout, varicosed legs of Emma Hedges with a sinuous twist of his supple body, but giving a chirrup of greeting as he did so.

Caroline had forgotten that this was one of the mornings when her

28

henchwoman arrived early, letting herself in with a key. It must be eight o'clock.

Mrs. Hedges, as usual, was carrying a shopping basket, which she had hung on the handle-bars of her ancient bicycle and which contained a rolled-up overall, a battered purse, house-shoes in a brown paper bag, and a copy of the Daily Mirror to read over her elevenses. She also carried this morning a folded copy of the Times, which she thrust at her employer.

"On the doorstep that was, Mrs. Lane," she said, in her rather clacking voice. "Too much trouble to put it through the letter-box. But that boy'll want his money all right. Why can't he do his job properly?"

She was a fierce worker herself, given to vigorous movement and speech, quick to censure the failings of the young, and greatly stimulated by the more sensational news items in her favourite journal.

"There doesn't seem much about the

murder in *your* paper," she remarked, as Caroline unfolded the Times. "At least, the headlines are all political."

She was too polite to express contempt for such a tame form of journalism, but her tone was condescending.

"Another murder?" said Caroline, not greatly interested, and glancing at the despised headlines as she followed the other woman to the kitchen.

"Yes, Mrs. Lane, and another and another it yet will be, till they bring back the rope," declared Mrs. Hedges, hanging her coat on a peg behind the door. "Strangled the poor woman was, in her own lounge, and left to lie, with the TV still on and tuned in to the commercials." Her tone suggested that the whole thing would have been less shocking if it had been a BBC programme.

"And *she* doesn't seem any better than she should be," she added sitting down and proceeding to change her shoes. "They're always the sort that get themselves murdered."

"Oh, but surely some quite decent, innocent people get murdered occasionally," protested Caroline.

"They're the sort that are what's called born victims," Emma instructed her, lifting an emcrimsoned face. "They kind of ask for it, without meaning to, if you know what I mean. Make things easy for the murderer to do them in. Won't see something fishy when it's staring 'em in the face."

Colonel mewed at the back door and she rose to let him in, drawing back the bolts noisily and closing the door with a bang when the cat had come running in.

"Starting to drizzle," she remarked gloomily, and took her overall out of the basket, replacing it with her hat, and hanging the whole on top of the coat on the back door.

"What was I saying?" she continued, buttoning the overall, while Caroline tipped some cat-food out of a tin onto a blue-ringed plate and put before her pet.

"You were talking about born victims," replied Caroline, feeling an inward shiver at the idea.

She filled the kettle and put it on the stove.

"Yes. But I was telling you about this murder that happened yesterday, Mrs. Lane," said Mrs. Hedges. "The police haven't got the one that done it yet, but, of course, they're looking for the husband. It's put tactful, mind you. Hoping he'll come forward and help 'em with some information, is how they put it. But naturally he's the man mostly likely to have done it, anyhow."

"Why?" asked Caroline.

"Why?" Emma turned prominent, pitying eyes on her lady. "Don't you know, Mrs. Lane, that the first thing the coppers think of when there's a murder is the husband done it, or the wife, as the case may be. Nine times out of ten they're right, too. Why, it's well known. Stands to reason, too."

"Does it?" said Caroline, as she cut

bread for toast. She was not enjoying the conversation, but it was hard to stop Mrs. Hedges in full spate, without giving offence.

"It does when you think about it, Mrs. Lane," said Emma, splashing hot water on to the piled up supper things in the sink. "There's no use denying married couples have some terrible rows at times. Begging your pardon, Mrs. Lane. I don't mean you and Mr. Lane do. But there, you're still newly-weds, aren't you. But when a violent sort of man loses his temper with his wife, you can see how he might go a bit too far. There's the scheming type, too, who fancies a bit of a change without no divorce. Maybe his wife's got a bit of money he'd sooner came to him than she took with her. Then there's the woman what can't stand her husband any more. He drinks, perhaps, or drugs. Or there's too much bed, or not enough, or she doesn't like the way he does it. Maybe it's just that he sniffs too much. Any way, she pops a bit of poison in his tea one day and that's that."

Caroline had made the tea and was attending to the toast. "But why couldn't she simply leave him?" she asked.

"Poisons easier, and she wants her widder's pension," said Mrs. Hedges, vigorously drying a cup. "Money comes into the ups and downs of marriage more than you might think Mrs. Lane.

"It sounds sordid and horrible," said Caroline, as she buttered the toast.

"Well, of course, I'm giving you the black side of marriage, Mrs. Lane," said Emma, putting two newly polished cups and saucers on the table. ("Yes, I will have a cup, thank you kindly.) I didn't think of such things myself when I'd been married not so much as a year, though my Bill was twenty-one years and five months older than me. Still is, of course. Only *then* it didn't seem to matter, and *now* I've got used to it. But there was a time in between — " She shook her head and sighed, as she dried her large red hands on the roller towel, before taking up the cup of tea Caroline had poured for her.

"Excuse me, Mrs. Lane, but is that all you're having?" she asked, eyeing the breakfast tray Caroline had prepared ready to take back to bed with her. "Wouldn't you like one of them nice newlaid brown eggs, or a bit of bacon?"

She knew that her employer seldom took more than toast and tea or coffee and a little fruit at this time, but she was hopeful that one morning Caroline would either abstain from this amount of nourishment or get herself a man size meal. Either extreme would be, in Mrs. Hedges's view a sign of pregnancy and she would have been delighted. If the doctors should discover complications, like twins or even triplets, or perhaps something wrong — but not too wrong — and all coming right in the end, she would have been still more pleased. She liked Caroline, but she needed drama, and got little enough of it first hand.

Caroline might have given her hope if she had admitted that she did feel rather sick that morning, but she could hardly explain that this was partly due to Mrs. Hedges own conversational powers. The discourse on marriage had somehow revived the doubt and uneasiness of the previous night.

In bed again, with the Times spread out and the hot tea to sip, life appeared brighter, however. Caroline imagined how, if Gordon had been home, she could have recounted Emma's views on the black side of marriage to him and they could have laughed together. She tried to laugh them away to herself, but she could not deny that there had seemed a horrible grain of truth in them at the time.

After her bath, she put on trousers, boots, anorak and headscarf, and, calling to her henchwoman, who was bumping the furniture about in the drawing-room now, that she was going for a 'breather' in the garden, went out into the drizzle.

From the garden she passed through a gate and took a path that led over a footbridge and along the further bank of the stream. The water moved sluggishly with only a whisper of sound and an occasional deep chuckle. The long slender branches of the willows hung moist and still, meeting their own reflections in the water. A vole swam silently across the stream, leaving a broadening wake of tiny ripples, and where the fringe of trees came to an end, swallows flew and dived above the surface, preparing for the long flight that lay ahead of them in the near future.

Soon Caroline ceased to notice these things as her mind gradually became engrossed in the interest and excitement of the book she was working on, hearing in her imagination an absorbing dialogue between two of the principal characters in it. It often happened like this on these solitary strolls of hers.

Retracing her steps slowly, she had reached the gate again when she became aware that Mrs. Hedges was gesturing wildly from outside the back door.

"Now what does she want?" Caroline muttered to herself, crossly and somewhat unfairly, loth to leave the private world of her own creating. But she began to hurry in spite of herself, affected by the urgency Emma always managed to convey.

"A caller," the daily announced, holding the door open for her employer's entry. "I've put him in the sitting-room, knowing you wouldn't be long. 'Mrs. Lane's gone for one of her little walks,' I told him. 'And bold it is of her to do so, with all them rapings and stabbing and I don't know what all, you read about. But I expect her back any minute.'"

"Is it somebody I know?" asked Caroline. "Didn't he give a name?" She felt a quick alarm, which Mrs. Hedges calmed with her apologetic reply.

"To tell you the truth, Mrs. Lane, I didn't quite get it, but it was sort of foreign sounding, and put me in mind of that German parson during the war. You know who I mean. It's on the tip of me tongue."

But as Caroline had only just been born when war broke out, and the name of the German pastor refused to leave Mrs. Hedges's tongue, she was none the wiser when, having dumped her anorak and scarf on a kitchen chair and run a comb through her hair, she asked for coffee and biscuits to be brought into the sitting-room.

She thought she knew who her visitor must be. A German who had been translating some of her books for publication in his own country, had mentioned to her agent that he was coming to England and hoped to meet her. It was unconventional of him to descend on Willow Lodge like this, without further warning, but she must try to make him feel welcome and hide her shyness as best she could.

She opened the sitting-room door with a little smile ready on her lips. But it switched off abruptly and her heart gave a leap of fear, as the red haired man she had seen on the doorstep the previous night, rose from a chair and stared penetratingly at her.

3

"**G**OOD morning. I hope I don't intrude." The words were polite enough, but they did not lessen Caroline's dismay.

What did the man want? Why was he so persistent?

"Mr. Fuller, my maid told me you gave her a foreign sounding name," she blurted accusingly.

His gaze wavered a little, but it could have been in surprise rather than confusion.

"Did she?" he said mildly. "I told her Neil Fuller. That's my genuine and lawful name, Mrs. Lane. There's nothing foreign sounding about Fuller, but perhaps Neil smacks of the Gaelic. I had a grandmother from the Scottish Highlands."

Knowing Mrs. Hedges's unreliability with names unfamiliar to her, Caroline began to feel foolish.

"Yes. Perhaps it was that," she said. "What is it you want, Mr. Fuller?" Then, her natural gentleness coming to the surface, added: "I'm sorry if I sound rude, but I'm rather busy this morning. If you want to see my husband, I'm afraid he's still away."

The memory of her deception the night before confused her a little, till she remembered his own deviousness over the phone.

"Do you mind if we sit down, Mrs. Lane. My business might take a little time," he said.

Every time he said her name he seemed to lay a slight but peculiar emphasis on it, she noticed with uneasiness and vague anger.

After a moment's hesitation, she sat down and indicated a chair for him opposite her but some little distance away.

He dropped into it, lessening the advantage he had held of superior height, but still looking physically dominant. There was an expression in his eyes that suggested he was thinking what to say, as he stared past her now at the sky beyond the window. Then he looked at her as if he had made up his mind about something.

"What do you know of your husband's affairs?" he asked abruptly.

She answered him cautiously: "Enough," And wondered if that was true. "Look," she said. "Wouldn't it be better to wait till my husband comes back. Or if your business really is urgent, get in touch with his firm. You see I can't give you his actual address at the moment. He moves about, you know. But his firm might be able to tell you. It's Dobson and Perks, and their offices are in Holborn. I suppose I should have told you that last night, but — "

"You pretended your husband had just gone down the road to the pub. Why did you do that, Mrs. Lane?" he said, eyeing her strangely. "What were you afraid of?"

She flushed. "You were a stranger — a man I'd never heard of — and I was alone in the house," she answered.

"I see," he said slowly, glancing away from her.

"And *you* knew Gordon was away when you rang, so why did you ask for him?" she said, counter attacking.

"To make sure he really was away," he said, frowning a little.

"Is that why you called, too?" she enquired, beginning to feel reassured, not noticing the ambiguous nature of his reply.

"No," he said, shaking his head. "I was sure by then."

"But — " she began, then broke off as Mrs. Hedges barged in carrying a lace covered tray, set with coffee-pot, milk jug, cups and saucers and some assorted biscuits arranged on a doyley covered plate.

"Coffee, madame," she said with the dignity of an old family retainer. Then spoilt the effect by adding: "There now! I've been and forgot the sugar."

Neil Fuller rose and took the tray from her large red hands and placed it beside the long stemmed Peace roses in the cut glass vase on the table.

"Much obliged, sir," said Emma, beaming at him, and scurried away to fetch the sugar.

Caroline arranged the coffee-cups. "Black or white, Mr. Fuller?" she asked in conventional tones.

"White, please. This is very good of you," he said looking, for the first time, slightly disconcerted.

She glanced doubtfully at him, but did not mention the German translator. Then, before she could pour the coffee, he had risen.

"I wonder if I might use your phone to make a call first," he said. "Do you know Dobson and Perks's number?"

"Not offhand," she answered, staring at him with the coffee-pot in hand, then putting it down. "But it will be in the London directory."

He stared back at her curiously. "You never ring your husband at the office, then?" he remarked.

"No. Mr. Dobson is old fashioned and objects," she told him. "Besides, I have no need."

"Not even when somebody wants him urgently, as I did — or said I did?" he asked.

She noticed the amendment. It was an admission in its way. What *was* it he wanted?

"Nobody has until now," she told him, and added: "And it's you who are going to make the call, not I."

He nodded at her. "That's right. But I don't see a telephone in the room."

"There's one in the hall and another in my writing-room, and an extension upstairs," she told him. "You'd better use the one in my writing-room. It's more private."

He nodded again. "Thank you. Perhaps you'll show me the way."

She rose and led him to the writing-room, having suggested he use the instrument there because of Mrs. Hedges long ears. It wasn't that

Emma deliberately eavesdropped. She just happened to be about when the phone was being used.

"Don't go, please," said Neil Fuller, as Caroline turned away from the desk. "This may be very important — to you, I mean."

"Very well. I'll stay," said Caroline, sitting down. "But I'd like to know *what* is so important, and how it concerns me."

"Of course. That's why I've asked you to stay," said the red headed man, turning the pages of a directory.

His finger travelled down a list of names and stopped. He muttered to himself, while Caroline wondered uneasily if she was falling victim to some sort of confidence trick or if there really was something vital to Gordon's interest and therefore her own in this call the stranger was about to make.

He perched on a corner of the desk while he made his contact, his eyes cast down, his brows creased in the faint frown she had noticed on his face before. This expression changed to one of keen alertness when a tinny little voice from the phone reached Caroline's ears.

"Hallo," said Neil. "I wonder if you can help me. I want to be put in immediate touch with a Mr. Lane who works for you. Yes, Lane. Mr. Gordon Lane."

Holding the receiver to his ear, he turned and gave Caroline a strange, bright-eyed stare as the tinny voice answered.

Then he said: "Are you sure of that? Look, would you be very kind and ask either Mr. Dobson or Mr. Perks if there isn't a Mr. Lane working for the firm? Oh well, Mr. Dobson then."

Caroline gave an exclamation and got up from the old armchair she had been sitting in.

"Yes, if you're the secretary you certainly ought to know," Neil was saying. "But just so that there can be no possible mistake, please ask Mr. Dobson. Yes, I'll hold on. Thank you very much."

"What did she say?" asked Caroline apprehensively.

He held a hand over the mouthpiece of the telephone.

"She says there is nobody called Lane working for Dobson and Perks. It's a very small firm and she is quite certain," he said in even tones.

"I don't believe her," said Caroline faintly. Or was it he who was lying?

He turned his attention back to the telephone.

"Hallo. Is that Mr. Dobson?" He beckoned Caroline near, and indicated that she should put her own head down to the instrument.

She did so, inhaling a faint odour of a pleasantly smelling after-shave lotion and the slightly rubbery smell of his water-proof jacket.

"My secretary tells me you're asking for a Mr. Lane," said a man's voice brusquely close to her ear.

"That's right. Mr. Gordon Lane," said Neil Fuller.

"Never heard of him. Sorry. Wrong firm, no doubt," said the voice, and there came the click of the receiver being replaced at the other end of the line.

Neil, too, replaced the telephone. He did not look at Caroline.

"There — there must be another Dobson and Perks," she said desperately.

"Look for yourself," he answered, with a wave of the hand towards the directory he had laid down.

She picked it up and searched the pages hopefully. But there was only one firm of exporters of the name she sought, and they were in Holborn as Gordon had said.

"I must have got it wrong," she said. "Perhaps Gordon's firm is Dobson and something else. Perhaps they don't call themselves exporters."

He looked at her then, and again with an expression that could have been compassionate.

"Search through all the Dobson's if you like and try every one, I think you'll get the same answer," he told her. "You're very loyal, aren't you. Or just content to go on being deceived. Yet you're not a stupid woman. You can't be. You've made quite a career for yourself in writing, they say." He glanced briefly at the shelf of books bearing the name, Carole Bannister on their spines. "Perhaps you're just a natural victim. There are such people."

Caroline started, remembering Mrs. Hedges's talk earlier that morning.

"I'm sorry. Perhaps I shouldn't have said that," Neil murmured.

He took her arm lightly and led her to the door. "Come and drink that coffee. I think you need it."

She went meekly with him into the hall and then suddenly stopped, asking herself what she was doing, why she was letting him lead her. Anger and hostility towards him surged up in her.

"Mr. Fuller, I think you've done

enough harm for this morning," she said jerking her arm away. "There's no doubt in my mind that you came here *meaning* to do harm. Well, it's done, so will you please go now. I'm sorry I can't offer you coffee after all."

Her anger drew sparks from him.

"If by 'harm' you mean helping you to climb out of a fool's paradise — if it really was any kind of paradise — then you're right," he declared. "If you want to stick your head back in the sand — "

"Aren't you mixing your metaphors?" Caroline interrupted. "But I'm neither an ostrich nor quite a fool, so will you please go."

"Not till I've warned you of the danger you may be running into if you remain deliberately blind," said Fuller, gravely now. "Let me tell you something about this man you've married."

"No," shouted Caroline, clapping her hands childishly over her ears. "Leave me. Go away."

He looked beyond her to where a broad red face crowned with grey brown hair peered round a door. Then he shrugged, marched to the front door, pulled it open, and hesitated, glancing back. But Caroline still stood with her hands covering her ears. He sighed and she heard the muffled slam of the door behind his back.

Her hands dropped to her sides. She went slowly into the sitting-room and sank into a chair.

"He's gone then," said Mrs. Hedges, in an odd voice, entering and staring round eyed at her employer. "I'll just take away the crocks, shall I? Why, you never ate none of the biscuits, Mrs. Lane. And here's your coffee not touched. Must be cold by now."

She gave another hard stare at Caroline.

"Are you all right?" she asked. "You don't look it. No, you don't, Mrs. Lane. Wouldn't you like to have a nice lie down?"

There was speculation mingled with

sympathy in her eyes. She had overheard what she thought of as a real old argy-bargy between her lady and the visitor, without being able to ascertain what it was all about. But it wasn't like Mrs. Lane to carry on the way she had been, shouting and covering her ears like one of the three monkeys on the mantel-piece. If she was in the family way it could account for it all right. There was no knowing how that might take a young woman, especially when it was her first.

Caroline forced a brief smile to her lips.

"I don't feel all that well, as a matter of fact," she admitted. "I wonder if you would mind heating up the coffee, and I think I'll have a teaspoonful of brandy in it. But I won't lie down, thank you."

"Put your feet up then," Mrs. Hedges advised. "I won't be a jiffy with the coffee and I'll get the brandy from the drinks cupboard and bring it all in together."

Caroline smiled again her agreement, knowing Emma's utter trust worthiness where drink was concerned. She had watched her own father drink away the rent money and sums that should have been spent on shoe repairs and warm clothing for herself, as a child.

The brandy did restore Caroline physically, though mentally she was still in a state of confusion and distress. Why had Gordon deceived her, she asked herself continually. And what exactly was the deception? Could he actually be working for Dobson and Perks after all, but under an assumed name? Or perhaps Lane was the assumed name. What had he been hiding? And what did Neil Fuller have to do with it?

She tactfully dismissed Mrs. Hedges, who was inclined to hover solicitously. She wanted to think clearly and logically and without interruption. First, she must make up her mind not to condemn Gordon unheard. After all, if she was as loyal as Neil Fuller had said, she would be finding now some perfectly good reason why her husband should have lied to her, even if it was only for her own peace of mind.

But what reason could there be? She closed her eyes tensely and tried to think. Suppose he was a secret agent, working for MI5 or MI6, or whatever it was, he might well find it impossible to tell her the truth, and his supposed job with Dobson and Perks could be just a cover.

Hope rose a little way, then fell as she examined this idea more closely. For one thing, Dobson and Perks had *not* covered for him. Surely even the most bungling of agents would have made sure of the firm's co-operation?

She walked restlessly about the room, wishing now she had not ordered the red headed man away before hearing what he had to say. She need not necessarily have believed it. But being left so much in the dark like this was almost worse than being given a hurtful explanation. At least she could have considered it, and rejected it if she had thought it was inspired by malice. Hadn't she told Neil Fuller to his face that he had come here to do harm?

And yet there had been a quite impressive air of sincerity about him at times. Perhaps he was a very good actor. Two things she was certain of. He had an old grudge against Gordon, for some reason. She could tell that by his manner when he mentioned her husband. There had been distaste and a hint of anger. And when he had phoned Dobson and Perks he had *expected* to be told that no Gordon Lane worked for them. He had not shown the least surprise.

Then another idea hit her. Of course! What a simple fool she had been! What proof was there that Fuller had in fact dialled Dobson and Perks's number? He could have rung some other firm and pretended it was the one he had said he would ring.

No, she told herself. He had mentioned the names Dobson and Perks quite clearly. He had asked to speak to

Mr. Dobson. But she had heard only his side of the conversation until the end. How could she be sure it was Mr. Dobson speaking? Hadn't the man — whoever it was — said something about the wrong firm?

Oh yes, she could hope after all. There was a great big doubt in her mind about the genuineness of that whole performance this morning. Only, if it had been all a pretence, what had been the object of it? There remained a mystery, but it must be that Neil Fuller had lied, not Gordon.

She hurried back to her writing-room, anxious to prove this conclusively. The directory was still open at the page both she and Fuller had consulted. But, when it came to the point, she hesitated with the receiver in her hand. Perhaps she feared to have hope snatched away from her at once, perhaps, as she thought, it was just that she had a better idea than to phone. She would go and visit Dobson and Perks at their offices in Holborn, taking a photograph of Gordon with her. That way there could be no doubt left in her mind as to the truth, one way or the other.

She replaced the receiver and went upstairs.

"I'm having lunch early, then going out," she told Mrs. Hedges, pausing in the doorway of the bathroom on the first floor.

"Going out?" repeated Emma, who had presented a broad behind to her employer as she gave a final polish to the bath. She turned round and rose erect.

"Do you think you ought, Mrs. Lane, when you feel so poorly?" she asked reproachfully.

"I'm much better now," Caroline told her. "And I've got to go to London. I shall take the car."

"Oh, to London!" said Mrs. Hedges, her face clearing.

She told herself that Mrs. Lane must be going to see a doctor this time, not a publisher. Naturally, she wanted one of the best, and all the top-notchers

were to be found in Harley Street
or round about, near the Zoo, so
you could take a look at the animals
afterwards and make a real day of
it.

4

HILDERS COURT was close to Holborn Circus, but Caroline had to stop the car and ask the way of several passers-by before finding one who knew it. It was dingy and quiet and old fashioned, and no doubt due for redevelopment. Not far away blocks of shining glass and concrete housed modern offices, staffed by workers as visible to the world as fishes in a pile of goldfish bowls. But No. 4, Hilders Court was more like a small ant-hill, closed and secretive. There was much more solid old brickwork to it than window space and from the pavement outside not a soul inside was visible.

She parked the Fiat at the kerb, hoping it would be obstructing nobody there. The stout outer door stood open and on either side were fixed the name-plates of the various firms that occupied the building. Dobson and Perks, Exporting Agents, were evidently on the first floor, on the right of the landing, with a detective agency above them, a firm selling something called Novelty Goods opposite and with storerooms below.

Caroline went slowly and hesitantly up the carpetless stairs, her courage and decision beginning to falter. She could hear the clacketing of a typewriter growing louder as she ascended. When she reached the gloomy landing she had half a mind to abandon her project, in her nervousness. But she told herself not to be a coward, that she had not come that far for nothing, and that whatever answer to her questions lay beyond the glass panelled door ahead, she must not run away from it. Most appropriately, under the name of the firm painted on the door was the word 'Enquiries'. She turned the handle and walked in.

The typewriter ceased its noise and the girl who was seated before it looked up with an unsmiling face. She had a pert nose and a discontented mouth. Her avalanche of hair was of no particular colour. It was obvious that she bit her nails.

The room was divided into offices by a partition of glass through which another woman was dimly visible, moving her head slowly from side to side as if reading or writing.

"Yes," said the typist ungraciously.

"Good afternoon," said Caroline. "My business is rather private. I would like to see the secretary, please, or Mr. Dobson preferably, if that's possible. There was a phone-call about it this morning."

"Oh yes," said the girl, eyeing Caroline up and down with a little more interest. "Well, you'll have to see Miss Pringle first at any rate. I suppose I'd better tell you I'm leaving to get married and not because I don't like the job, though I'm not saying I'd stay on permanent even if we wasn't moving to Leeds on account of my boy-friend's work."

"Oh, really?" said Caroline, taken aback at this confidence, "Well, I hope you'll be very happy, but — "

"Thanks. They say you should try everything once, don't they," said the girl, pushing back her hair and getting up, revealing the most mini of mini-skirts. Then she crossed to a door in the glass partition and opened it, beginning a murmured conversation with the woman beyond.

Glancing round her, Caroline noticed another door in the wall to the right, evidently leading to a back room and marked 'Private'.

"What name was it, please?" asked the typist, reappearing.

"Lane," said Caroline. "Mrs. Lane."

"Do come this way, Miss Lime," invited the woman in the inner office, appearing in the open doorway.

She was slender and very neat, with beautifully arranged blonde hair, a comparatively aged face and a smile that did not reach her eyes. These eyes seemed somehow less important than her fashionably styled spectacles.

"The agency did ring us this morning to say that someone was coming," she remarked. "But I understood that the name was Price. I'm Miss Pringle. Do sit down, Miss — er — "

"Mrs. Lane," said Caroline. "And I'm afraid I don't know what you mean by the agency. What agency?"

The secretary looked at her more sharply.

"Haven't you come about the typing job?" she asked.

"No," answered Caroline. "Certainly not. I've come about a phone-call that was made to you this morning. But first I want to ask if it *was* in fact made to you. This may seem odd, but I have a reason for asking. Did a man ring up and ask to be put in touch with a Mr. Lane? Mr. Gordon Lane?"

She waited anxiously while Miss Pringle stared silently through the distinguished spectacles.

"Yes," she said slowly, at last.

"There was such a call. I told the man who phoned that there wasn't anybody called Lane on the firm, or connected with it. He didn't believe me, or pretended not to. I had to put him through to Mr. Dobson. I hope *his* word was considered good enough."

Her head jerked a little and there was a touch of offence in her tone, but she was curious, too, as was evident by the way she continued to stare at Caroline.

"Please, Miss Pringle, don't think *I'm* doubting your word," she said. "I'm not, but — but would it be possible for me to speak to Mr. Dobson personally? Or perhaps Mr. Perks."

"Mr. Perks isn't here," declared Miss Pringle, still staring.

It had occurred to Caroline that her idea that Gordon might be engaged on some sort of secret work need not be so far fetched after all, because though Dobson and Perks could be used as a cover, Miss Pringle might not know this. And how could Mr.

66

Dobson have told Neil Fuller that Mr. Gordon Lane did in fact work for them if the secretary was listening and knew very well that he didn't?

The secretary stood up abruptly, adjusting her spectacles as if to give herself moral support.

"I'll see if Mr. Dobson is engaged," she said, with no hint of encouragement in her tone.

Caroline got up and followed her quietly to the door marked 'Private,' but before either could reach it, it opened abruptly and a man looked out.

He was tall and thin, with a yellowish skin and full dark eyes. His hair was black and dry looking, but quite thick for a man nearing fifty. His good grey suit was well brushed, but not very new. Pinned to a lapel was a perfectly shaped dark red rose.

As she stared at this, Caroline heard again in imagination Gordon saying: "There's one thing about old Dobson. He's not a ray of sunshine, but he loves flowers. Always wears a rose in his coat. Grows them himself. He's potty about his garden and greenhouse. They're wife and children to him. He's a bachelor with a dragon of a housekeeper."

She stepped forward quickly.

"Mr. Dobson?" she said. "Could I speak to you privately, please? I won't keep you long, but it's very important."

He glanced reproachfully at Miss Pringle, who was hovering uncertainly now. The typist watched with covert interest, while pretending to be fully occupied with the document she was copying.

"Er — what's it about?" asked Dobson cautiously.

"It's to do with that phone-call this morning asking for a Mr. Lane," the secretary told him. "I've told this lady that there's nobody of that name here."

"That's so," said Mr. Dobson.

His choleric dark eyes had a look of surprise and curiosity in them as they met Caroline's pleading gaze. "But it

68

was a man who phoned, wasn't it?" he added.

"Yes," said Caroline. "Please, will you let me explain?"

The sight of that rose had filled her with hope again, for here, she thought, was evidence that Gordon had some genuine connection with this man, Dobson. On the other hand, the exporting agent seemed really puzzled.

He glanced a little ostentatiously at his gold wristwatch. "I'm afraid I can't spare more than a few minutes," he said. "Hurry up with those Argentine papers, will you, Miss Pringle, or Da Silva's man will be on the phone again."

"Sonia is doing the final typing now, Mr. Dobson," said the secretary eagerly.

Her employer nodded unsmilingly and stood back for Caroline to precede him into the inner office.

It was a fair sized room with two desks in it, two lockers and a large filing cabinet. In front of the dingy window, with its close-up view of the backs of buildings, was a row of indoor plants, flourishing surprisingly.

Mr. Dobson waved Caroline to a chair in front of the desk that was situated nearest to these, and sat down behind the desk himself. It was paper-strewn and needed dusting. The room itself smelt of dust, as well as stale tobacco. There was a cigar butt in an ashtray among the papers.

"My partner isn't here at the moment," said the exporter, seeing Caroline glance towards the second desk.

She remembered Gordon telling her that Perks was usually abroad some-where, making connections and pursuing business.

"Now what can I do for you, Mrs. — er — Do you smoke?"

She shook her head at the silver cigarette-case he held open for her, but did not give her name again.

"I'm making some enquiries about a man called Gordon Lane," she said nervously.

"Oh yes? And how can I help?" he said, taking a cigarette for himself and lighting it efficiently with a lighter that matched the case.

"I — I know you said this morning that you don't know the name, but it has occurred to me that you may know *him* all the same, but not as Gordon Lane, and so — " She flushed a little as she broke off and began searching in her bag for the envelope containing the snapshot of Gordon which she had placed there before setting out.

She got it out and dropped it. It went under the desk, and he courteously reached for it with a long arm and handed it back to her. But he glanced at the direction as he did so, and Caroline knew he must have read her name. He stared at her a little oddly, his sallow face flushed with stooping now.

"This is all very mysterious," he said. "Would you mind making yourself a bit clearer. You think I might know the man you're looking for under another name? Is he a crook of some sort?"

"Oh no," said Caroline quickly, confused at the suggestion. "At least — no I'm sure he isn't."

With fingers that trembled slightly, she pulled the snapshot out of the envelope and handed it to him.

"That's him," she said simply, and watched his face as he took it and frowned over it in silence.

She had taken the photograph herself, from her writing-room window, with a telescopic lense fixed to her camera, when Gordon had been standing on the lawn staring up at some passing pigeons, looking as if he wished he had his gun with him. He had not known he was being taken. He still did not know, for the prints had arrived only recently, during his absence, and she was hoping to surprise him with them. The snap was in colour and showed his healthy tan, light blue eyes and blond hair, which had been boyishly ruffled by the breeze. It was a good likeness.

72

"Do you know him?" Caroline blurted.

Mr. Dobson shook his head and handed the print back to her with nicotine stained fingers.

"No," he said. "He's nobody I deal with, as far as I know."

"Oh," said Caroline, disappointed. "And he really doesn't work here?"

"No. You've already been told that," said the exporter, frowning again. "Now, if you'll excuse me — "

"Yet *he* knows *you*," said Caroline, desperately. "He has told me all sorts of things about you. You'd be surprised at the things he knows."

She was quite unprepared for his reaction to her innocent statement. A look of fury suddenly flooded his full dark eyes.

"You dirty little blackmailer!" he exclaimed, in a low tone that suggested he was making an effort to control his anger. "You've got nothing on *me*. Get out before I ring for the police."

Horrified, Caroline could only sit

and gape at him for a moment. Then she stammered: "Oh no. I didn't mean — Mr. Dobson, you're making a terrible mistake. Surely you can't really think I was trying to blackmail you. I didn't mean that Gordon had told me harmful things about you, only about your plants, and that you always wore a button-hole and loved your garden and your greenhouse, and — and — " Here, as she remembered that her husband had also mentioned that old Dobson had a quick temper, a worse horror came upon her, and she found herself shedding tears.

In a moment he was beside her, patting her shoulder gently, though he made a great noise in getting up and round the desk, so that she thought for a moment he might be going to assault her.

"I'm sorry, my dear, I'm sorry," he murmured anxiously. "I do apologize. Only your approach was a little — eh? Shall I ring for Miss Pringle? A glass of water, eh?"

"No thank you," said Caroline, gulping and drying her eyes. "I'll go. I didn't mean to make such a fool of myself. It's I who should apologize really. Please forgive me."

She managed to smile at him, as she rose, and met a look of quick sympathy that was very different from his previous expression.

"This fellow you're looking for, has he harmed you in some way?" he asked gruffly.

"Oh no," answered Caroline, putting away her handkerchief with a final sniff. "I expect it's just a misunderstanding and will all be explained when he comes home."

"He's your husband?" said the exporter.

She nodded. "Yes."

"I'm sorry," he murmured.

"Oh, it's not so bad as that," she said, trying to laugh. "Just something a bit puzzling. *I'm* sorry — to have troubled you like this."

"Shall I call a taxi for you?" he asked kindly.

"No, thank you. I have my car outside," she told him, walking to the door. "Goodbye."

"Goodbye, Mrs. — er Lane. I wish I could have helped you," he returned, opening the door for her and gazing at her with interest and concern, as she went out.

She walked through the outer office without glancing at Sonia, eyeing her above the typewriter, or Miss Pringle, frankly staring behind her screen of glass, where she existed rather like a withering hothouse flower herself.

Caroline drove home no happier than when she had set out, if a little wiser. But she doubted if wiser was quite the word, asking herself in some bitterness whether it might not have been better if she had let well alone. She could have comforted herself then with the suspicion that Neil Fuller had tricked her in some way with that phone call. And what did it matter, after all, what Gordon really did for a living, or what firm he worked for?

But she could not sustain this mood. She knew too well that it mattered very much that her husband had deceived her and lied to her fluently and convincingly. And it was hard to avoid the conclusion that he had done this because he was ashamed of the truth about himself or thought, at least, that she would greatly disapprove of it.

Could he be doing something criminal? How she wished her faith in Gordon was strong enough for her to dismiss such an idea entirely from her mind. But this she couldn't do.

When she was free at last from the area of densely packed houses and High Streets and shopping centres, each one almost exactly like the last, she pulled the Fiat up against a green hedge along a quieter road and switched off the engine. A pony came and blew down its nose at her on the other side of the hedge, and in a copse further along the road a wood pigeon cooed languorously.

There she sat and allowed her mind

to travel back to the time when she had first met the man she had married.

It had been at Scarborough. She had gone there because a room had been booked for her in a hotel favoured by Aunt Lilian, who had then no idea that she was about to die before the planned holiday with her goddaughter could take place. It had been a curious kind of apathy that had made Caroline retain the booking for herself, while cancelling Aunt Lilian's. She needed a holiday, so why bother to think up anywhere else to go, she had asked herself.

She knew now that she had been very unenterprising. The truth was she had been associating so much with elderly people that she had grown to think like they did. While living at home with her father and mother she had worked as part-time secretary to an octogenarian General who was writing his memoirs, and did her own writing when she could. Later, after the death of her parents — both in their early seventies, she had gone to live with her ageing godmother, and devoted her time to getting really established as a successful author.

It was in Scarborough that her loneliness had become really apparent to her. In a way, the private world she had created in her books had provided her with both adventure and young companionship. But in the big hotel, isolated among a crowd of eager holiday makers, she knew how short she was of both in real life.

Then, on her third day there, Gordon had appeared and asked if he might share her table in the tea-lounge. His manner had been appealingly diffident, and she had been glad to assent. In no time at all, it seemed, they were talking away like old acquaintances.

He confided that he had been living in South America for some years and felt out of touch with modern England. He was, he said, a stranger in his own country, and a lonely one at that. She confessed to a similar feeling, though without the excuse of having lived abroad, and he expressed a flattering surprise. In some subtle way he made her feel attractive and desirable — even exciting. When he had asked her to give him some of her company during her stay in Scarborough, where he was lodged at a guesthouse on a semi-permanent basis, she had agreed at once.

It had been during a delightful picnic on the moors that he had hinted at the reason for his leaving England in the first place. There had been a woman. He had been in love with her. They were practically engaged. Then she had died in tragic circumstances, drowning somewhere off the coast of Brittainy, when on holiday with her family. His parents were dead and he was an only child, so he had tried to run away from his grief and frustration. It had been rather corny perhaps — like big game hunting in Africa or joining the Foreign Legion, he had ended with a shrug and rueful little laugh, but that was the way it had been.

In exchange she had given him an account of her own life and the circumstances that had brought her to Scarborough and had soon found herself telling him about Willow Lodge and her decision not to sell it.

"Won't you be lonely, living there all by yourself?" he had asked, and had added: "But of course, you'll marry." Then, half teasingly, but looking her in the eyes, he had said: "I wouldn't mind being the lucky man myself."

Immediately he had changed the subject to a house he had lived in for a time in Rio, with an American couple who had treated him like a son.

He had left her that night pleasantly disturbed, wondering just how much he had meant by that remark. She began to consider him as a possible husband, though she had never really been anxious to marry. He was certainly a satisfactory holiday companion. But, of course, that wasn't enough. He was not exactly handsome, but there was an odd, almost magnetic charm about him. Was she, perhaps, falling a little in love with him? Nonsense, she told herself. And in any case, he was probably not the kind of man to fall for her. She had better be careful and watch herself.

But that was before he had kissed her. To Caroline, who had experienced only the clumsy embraces of a fellow teenager when she was seventeen, and the furtive pawings — hurriedly discouraged — of a middle-aged admirer in a literary class she had once attended for a term, that kissing had been a revelation and a late awakening. Before the holiday was over she was engaged to Gordon. The Registry Office wedding had followed only five weeks later.

The anniversary of that first meeting had just passed, and she and her husband had celebrated with champagne and a special dinner. Not in a restaurant, however. Gordon hadn't favoured that idea of hers, saying that he had enough of London when he had to go there for business and anywhere on the South Coast was overcrowded. Besides, its was cosier and cheaper to stay at home — more romantic too, really, with just the two of them alone together.

These reflections brought a vivid picture of Gordon before Caroline's mind. His curious way of smiling without parting his lips, his blond hair that she couldn't help suspecting he kept that way by artificial means, though once she had accepted his story that it had been bleached by the South American sun. His ordinary face that seemed transformed to something more than ordinary when he chose to exert his own peculiar charm, and that could seem downright unattractive in other moods of his, when his blue eyes would become cold and pale, his lips thin and his whole personality would seem to shrivel in some odd way.

But tomorrow he would be at his best. He always was when he returned after one of his business trips. How would he react, though, when she taxed him with his deceitfulness? She must try to be restrained and choose her words. She must not put him into one of those queer, shut-in, cold-eyed moods. She admitted to herself that when he was like that she was actually repelled by him — even a little afraid of him.

5

WEDNESDAY dawned fine and sunny, though the night before had been wet and windy. Caroline had lain awake for some hours, listening to the rain beating on the bedroom windows and running down the gutters, to the accompaniment of a curiously musical droning in the old chimneys, rather like a giant blowing on a gigantic flute. Later she slept fitfully and dreamed vaguely unpleasant dreams.

When she finally woke, however, and saw the sunshine and heard the robin that was singing under the windows, her spirits lightened a little. Perhaps, she thought, she had been exaggerating the importance of her discovery about Gordon. There might be some fairly simple explanation after all. It could be that her husband's real job was so much more humble than he had pretended, that false pride had made him lie to her. Childish behaviour, maybe, but not criminal. Whatever the truth it seemed likely that his actual employers must have some connection with Dobson and Perks and he had heard the exporter talked about.

She bathed and dressed with more than usual care, putting fresh varnish on her nails and clipping on a pair of jade earrings Gordon had once admired, though she did not expect him home until fairly late in the day. It was just possible, though, that he would take a night train from Newcastle, in which case he might be arriving at any time that morning.

Then she reminded herself that there was no certainty that he had been any where near Newcastle, that she had no idea at all where he had been spending this past week.

It was moments of truth like this that gave her impulses quite different from her plan to be tactful and gentle with her husband on his return, and she knew that when she did face him it would be a question whether impulse or design would win.

After breakfast, while Mrs. Hedges — secretly disappointed that her lady had told her nothing of yesterday's trip to London — plied the vacuum cleaner in the writing-room, Caroline made ready to go to the shops. She was planning porterhouse steak for dinner, to be garnished with mushrooms and served with salad. And they could try those grilled bananas with caramel sauce, she decided. For lunch, cauliflower with cheese sauce would do.

She had not been much of a cook when she married, but she had learned fast. She still didn't bother much with her new skill when she was alone, however.

Thinking of these practical domestic matters gave her the illusion that all was well and she had made no shattering discovery; that she was just an ordinary wife preparing to welcome home an ordinary husband, on his return from a humdrum business trip. But it did not last long.

Fortunately she had to keep her attention on her driving once she had reached the High Street, for though only a small town — little more than a large village, in fact Oxridge had plenty of traffic. A favourite route to the coast ran through it, and there were two bottle-necks, one where a narrowing road crossed the stream and one where a handsome old building protruded.

There were a few familiar faces to smile at and wave to in passing and when she had reached the butcher's shop, Caroline found another acquaintance taking up a good deal of room in the small place. This was Mrs. Harding, who got up the local flower-shows and had known Aunt Lilian. She turned from pointing at a shoulder of lamb with a horny finger and creased her broad face amiably at sight of her old friend's goddaughter.

"Hallo. You're looking a bit peaked, my dear," she said. Must be all that writing. You need to get out in the garden a bit more. Not really a gardener, are you?"

"Well, no. Not really," said Caroline deprecatingly.

"Leave it to hubby, do you?" said Mrs. Harding. "I suppose he'll be staking those chryanthemums now he's back again."

"Oh dear! They do need doing, I'm afraid," said Caroline, thinking guiltily of the neglected plants rampant near the front gate of Willow Lodge. "We really need a part-time gardener. But it's like asking for the moon. My husband isn't exactly an enthusiast, either, you see, but perhaps when he comes home — I'm expecting him today."

Mrs. Harding's two chins dropped slightly, and she gave Caroline a curious stare.

"You mean he's not — But I thought — " she said.

"Your meat, madam," said the butcher, thrusting a polythene wrapped parcel at her. "Did I hear you mention chrysanthemums? When's the show to be? Do you want me to stick up a poster like I did last year?"

Mrs. Harding was instantly side-tracked and, while Caroline gave her order, lingered to hold a dialogue with the butcher on the probable glories to be seen shortly in the church hall and the chances of local gardeners in open competition. She went out, finally, without having finished or explained those broken sentences Caroline's statement about Gordon's homecoming seemed to have surprised from her. But Caroline thought little about them, having enough mystery to worry over already.

Her husband had not returned by one o'clock and she ate cauliflower in cheese sauce at the kitchen table, with only Colonel for company, Mrs. Hedges having gone home to sausages and chips with her ageing husband.

In the afternoon she tried to write, but it was almost impossible to concentrate. There was very little traffic on the road that passed the house and each infrequent car made her pulses jump, as she imagined it was her husband approaching. But at half past four he still had not arrived.

The warmth and sunshine tempted her to carry her tea into the garden, and she sat in a folding chair facing the willows, with a tray on a stool beside her and Colonel at her feet. The cat lapped from a saucer of milk while his mistress drank two cups of tea slowly and felt the sun seeping into her with its end-of-summer benevolence. Once she gazed at the already thinning willows and thought she saw a figure slip quickly behind one of them. Something furtive in the movement alarmed her. Something odd about the shape, too, for it seemed to her to have an abnormally large head.

She put down her teacup and stood up to see better. But though she stared watchfully for some little time she saw nobody and nothing unusual. Could it have been a trick of light that had disturbed her? Or had she imagined the incident out of sheer nerves?

She went back to the house even less inclined to work on her book and eventually occupied herself with odd jobs till it was time to prepare dinner. Once the phonebell rang and Caroline went to answer it with mixed feelings of apprehension and relief. If it should be Gordon — But it was only another acquaintance of Aunt Lilian's to invite her to a coffee morning in aid of Oxfam.

She postponed actually cooking the dinner till nine o'clock, then grilled half the steak for herself with a tomato and a couple of mushrooms and ate it with some crisp bread, finishing off with an apple. It would not take long to grill the other half of the steak for Gordon when he came.

But by midnight he had not come.

Her evening had been spent uneasily

in snatches of viewing and snatches of reading and a great deal of listening for Gordon's Vauxhall.

At twelve she went to bed, nervously exhausted, and passed the night in troubled dreams and sudden wakings.

The next day, Thursday, was almost a repetition of Wednesday, except that she did not go to the shops, and Mrs. Hedges expressed a mild surprise that Mr. Lane had not returned as expected, then talked a good deal about the operation for gallstones recently performed on a friend of hers and the trouble her cousin was having with a teenage daughter.

The afternoon was overcast and still and a deckchair in the garden did not seem inviting. Besides, Caroline could not go on neglecting her work indefinitely. The book had been going so well until now, too. But it was extremely difficult, she found, to get back into the England of the thirteenth century and the problems of her young hero and heroine, when her own life faced her with such a poser. She tried, however. She tried for nearly four hours.

At the end of that period she crossed out all that she had forced herself to write, finding, on reading through it, that it was unconvincing and seemed mere padding.

When darkness began to gather and the last of the few home-going motorists who came that way had driven past, a great silence seemed to settle over the house. A feeling of being alone and abandoned mastered Caroline briefly. She had a strange unreasoning conviction that her husband was not returning that night — or indeed ever, that Gordon had gone out of her life for good.

She pulled herself out of the mood by an effort of will, and told herself that such a notion was nonsence. Gordon had said quite plainly that he was coming back on Wednesday. So he was a day late. What of it? If it should turn out that he was two or even three days late it would be no great matter.

Only, why didn't he phone? Surely she would have been notified if he had been taken ill or had been involved in an accident.

Suppose he had taken offence because she had been making enquiries about his work behind his back, and was punishing her now by keeping her in this suspense. But that was an absurd idea! How could he possibly know?

But it was partly the thought of punishment, as well as a weariness with her own company, that made her decide suddenly to go to the Hand in Hand that evening, instead of waiting meekly at home to welcome her husband when he should choose to present himself.

It was just under a mile to the public house, but she got out the Fiat to drive there. She left the porch light burning and the kitchen light shining down on a note laid open on the table. It said: 'Hallo, darling. Thirsty and forlorn, so gone to the Hand in Hand for a while. Love C.'

Would he come and find her? Or

ring to tell her he was home? Better perhaps if their reunion was in public, she thought, as she put a reluctant Colonel outside and bolted the back door, with a brief remembrance of the figure she had seen — or fancied she had seen — lurking among the willows the day before.

The Hand in Hand was a pleasant little inn, tile-hung and set well back from the road, with a couple of benches outside and a pollarded elm in the forecourt, beside which a few cars were already parked. A hum of conversation in mainly masculine voices greeted Caroline, as she pushed open the door of the Saloon Bar and entered. She felt ridiculously shy, for she had scarcely been inside a public house at all before her marriage and had never visited one unescorted since. Sometimes, on a Saturday evening, she and Gordon had called in here for a drink and a chat with one or two of the regulars, and the landlord and his wife.

Tonight, neither the Gleesons, from the Clock and Watchmakers shop in the High Street, nor the Pounds, who owned the Rose Nursery, or old Edward Ball, the retired barrister, was present. One or two men whose faces she knew vaguely gave her nods and murmured greetings, and a woman with one of them smiled in friendly fashion. Only Mimi Eccles behind the bar, with her wig-like hair and pink face, her brooch-decorated bosom straining at her light blue dress, gave her a warm welcome.

"Hallo there, Mrs. Lane. Mr. Lane not home yet?"

"No not yet," answered Caroline, feeling slightly more confident.

She heard the door open and close and turned, heart giving a little leap. But of course there would not have been time for Gordon to get to Willow Lodge, read her note and come on here. It was only an unknown young man in a crash helmet who entered. She had an idea he had been coming along behind her as she drove from home.

She ordered a glass of sherry and stood at the counter sipping it for a little while, hoping that Mrs. Eccles would keep up her meaningless chatter about the weather, but the landlady soon deserted and began a playful conversation with a stocky man in a tweed hat.

Carrying her drink to a small table between the two windows, Caroline sat quiet and watchful, scarcely tasting the indifferent wine. Everybody else seemed to be engrossed in conversation and easy companionship. Everybody else except the motor-cyclist who had followed her in. She wondered why he didn't remove the scarf that hid his chin as well as his throat. No doubt it had been highly suitable for speeding through the autumn evening outside, but must surely be too warm for indoor wear.

Next moment, he turned quickly from his survey of the room and faced the counter again, she wondered if she had been staring too openly. Then, happening to glance at the gay appearance of the bottles on the shelves behind the bar, she noticed with surprise that his eyes, reflecting in the mirror that hung there too, seemed to be fixed unwaveringly upon herself.

Her shyness returned as she wondered if he could possibly be planning to approach her. Perhaps he thought she had come there alone expressly for the purpose of picking up a man. Some women did, she believed, though hardly in such a very respectable pub as the Hand in Hand. Well, she must assist him to get rid of the idea, if he had it.

She looked at her watch as if expecting a friend who was late, and frowned slightly.

And then the door opened and at sight of the man who entered she caught her breath sharply and felt a faint tingling shock of apprehension. It was Neil Fuller.

He did not see her sitting alone at the little table, for the back of his head was turned towards her as he shut the door. He glanced round him as he walked to the bar, but still his gaze did not reach her. The motor-cyclist made way for him at the counter and he ordered a drink. It was Mimi Eccles, smiling and patting her blonde beehive of hair, who pointed out where Caroline was sitting, as Neil put down the money for his beer.

He turned then with a startled face, while the motorcyclist buried his face in his own tankard as if demonstrating his lack of interest.

Neil carried his drink across to the little table, pulled out a chair and sat down without asking her permission. All the time his eyes never left her face.

"Hallo," she said, trying to hide her nervousness and appear at ease, conscious that Mrs. Eccles was giving her speculative looks as she polished a glass.

"You're alone?" he said, without returning her greeting.

"Yes," she said, fingering her sherry glass.

"Didn't your husband come home yesterday?" asked Neil in a low voice, leaning across the table towards her and maintaining his watchful gaze on her.

"No," answered Caroline, darting a quick upward glance at him. "He's not back yet."

"And you don't know where he is, do you?" said Neil with a little nod, as if he knew the answer to that without being told.

Caroline bit her lip, then gave him back stare for stare as she asked bluntly: "Do you?"

His eyes wavered and he lifted his beer. "No," he said and took a large sip. "Why should you think I do?" he added.

"Because you seem to know more about him than I do," she murmured with some bitterness. Somehow she had lost her nervousness. "You knew Gordon didn't work for Dobson and Perks before you phoned them," she accused.

Neil hesitated, then answered cautiously: "Let's say that I thought it highly unlikely that he was employed by them." He leaned towards her again. "Look, we can't talk properly here. When you've finished your drink perhaps we could take a little walk outside, or sit in my car and discuss this."

"We'll sit in mine," Caroline told him firmly.

She did not trust him. In fact, her recent discovery had made her doubtful of almost everybody for the time being. Perhaps it was naive to imagine there was any security in sitting behind the steering wheel of her Fiat to talk to Neil, but she felt that it was safer than roaming about in the dark with him, or entering his own car.

It was night now, but the lamp outside the public house illuminated the sign that depicted two clasped hands, one delicately female and the other sturdily male, and made light enough to see by, as Caroline unlocked the door of her car on the driving side and leaned across to release the lock on the opposite door. She could see that a smallish car painted in tan and cream had been added to the row of cars parked outside. Presumably this belonged to Neil.

She felt a stirring of curiosity about him. She wondered what his job was and whether he was married and had a family. He was, she judged, about her own age, thirty-four. She studied him covertly while he settled beside her in the front seat of the Fiat. His face wore a rather grim expression, but she had an idea this was not normal to it.

They sat in silence for a moment. Caroline had parked the car to face the entrance of the Saloon, and now she saw the motor-cyclist come out, fastening his crash helmet and pulling up his scarf. He stood looking round in a hesitating manner, and she turned her glance discreetly away, imagining he was looking for a plain-to-see notice depicting a hand pointing round the side of the building and saying simply: 'Gents'.

"Well?" she said quietly. "Aren't you going to tell me why you thought it so unlikely my husband was working for Dobson and Perks?"

Equally quietly Neil answered: "Because they were people I was sure he'd want to avoid, since he had changed his name and appearance a little from the days when he had a slight connection with them."

"Changed his name?" exclaimed Caroline, more loudly than she had intended. She glanced round the forecourt and saw that the motor-cyclist had walked to his machine at the end of the row of cars and appeared to be examining it. "I don't believe it," she declared in a lowered tone, not quite sincerely.

"When I knew your husband five or six years ago he was calling himself George Longton," said Neil. "And he wore a small beard. Most distinguished, the women thought it," he added sarcastically.

She told herself that she need not accept this as the truth. That he could so easily be lying. She gave an unconvincing little laugh.

"You've mistaken Gordon for somebody else," she said. "For one thing, you say he did have some connection with Dobson and Perks, yet Mr. Dobson never recognized him when I showed a snapshot of my husband."

"I don't think Dobson ever knew George Longton very well," Neil said, unmoved. "And without the beard — " He shrugged. "So you went to see him," he added, with a curious look.

She nodded, then challenged him: "How well did *you* know this George Longton, anyway? *And* how well do you know my husband?"

But she was finding the air of scepticism increasingly hard to maintain, because, after all, she herself had thought of the possibility of Gordon having changed his name.

Neil appeared to hesitate again. Then he answered: "George Longton was my brother-in-law, and from my observation of your husband I have no doubt that he's the same person."

"But Gordon was an only child, like me. He told me so," said Caroline stupidly, then saw the fallacy of this reasoning. "But I suppose you'll say that was a lie, too," she added in a tone that sounded forlorn even to her own ears.

"It doesn't really matter whether he was an only child or not," Neil told her patiently. "I'm trying to tell you that he was once married to my sister."

"Oh!" said Caroline, and for a moment found words fail her. Then she stammered: "But Gordon — " and broke off, biting her lip again.

"Said he was a bachelor. I've no doubt of it," said Neil dryly.

"What happened?" muttered Caroline, after a pause.

"She died," said Neil. "She was drowned, while on holiday, in Brittainy."

"Oh, I see," said Caroline. And for a moment she thought she did. "Gordon told me about her," she explained. "At least, he didn't say she was actually his wife. Perhaps he couldn't bear to. But he did tell me of a girl he once loved who was drowned while on holiday with her family, and it was off the coast of Brittainy."

Perhaps, she thought, it had affected his mind in some way, and caused him to try to hide in another personality. It could all be explained psychologically, and poor Gordon really wanted help, not censure.

"My sister, Rosalind, was on holiday with *him*, alone, and most reluctantly," said Neil, bitterly. "She'd seen through him and wanted to leave him. He persuaded her to have one last try to make a go of the marriage. That was how he put it. I advised against it, when she confided in me, but he talked her round."

"You sound so bitter about it," Caroline murmured, while she considered this previous marriage of her husband's and wondered half jealously how much it had meant to him. "Surely it was a tragedy for him as much as for anybody!" Why had Neil said Rosalind had seen through him? What had she seen?

"It was most *convenient* for him," said Neil, answering her spoken remark. "Rosalind had money of her own and it all went to him by a will she would certainly have changed if she had lived."

Caroline made a small shocked sound at the implication.

"It was money awarded her in a car accident," Neil continued. "She lost an arm you see."

Caroline gave another exclamation.

"She used to think it would put the young men off her. She was a diffident person to begin with," Neil went on. "It made it easier for Longton to get her."

"Oh, it would," thought Caroline, remembering her own shyness and the skill with which Gordon had overcome it.

"I told her she was making a mistake, when she married him," said Neil. "But I couldn't warn her it would be the death of her."

"But — what you suggested — that it was convenient for him that she died — it's monstrous!" faltered Caroline. "As if he didn't care so long as he got the money!"

Her voice had risen again.

"Ssh!" muttered Neil. "That chap with the motor-bike will hear. *I* don't mind who listens, but *you* have to live in these parts."

Caroline realized that the young man had wheeled his machine out of the row and was crouched in front of it tinkering with the front light.

"You think I'm doing Longton an injustice?" Neil went on in a low voice, speaking with a controlled bitterness still. "Let me tell you just how she met

109

her death, my sister. Her husband took her out in a dinghy, when the sky was overcast and bad weather threatened, and nobody in their senses would have thought of going for a nice row."

"She didn't have to go," Caroline pointed out. "She must have wanted to, herself."

"You didn't know my sister," said Neil. "She had agreed to give the marriage a last chance. She wouldn't have risked a quarrel with Longton over a mere trip in a dinghy. He went in for cold sulks when thwarted."

'Like Gordon,' thought Caroline, then reminded herself that it *was* Gordon Neil was talking about.

"Besides, Rosalind liked the sea," he continued, "though she couldn't swim. We only had Longton's account of what happened. There were no witnesses. He said that her scarf blew away, they tried to reach it and, between them upset the boat which was rocking a bit by then, anyway, as the weather had worsened. He managed to cling to the upturned dinghy, when he surfaced, but Rosalind had been swept away by a big wave, evidently hampered by her lack of two arms. He tried to reach her, but was seized with cramp and nearly drowned himself. He was discovered still clinging to the boat when a rescue party reached it after they had been missing some time. There was no sign of my sister by then. When her body did eventually turn up, it was hard even to identify her, let alone say how she had died."

"How horrible!" exclaimed Caroline, with a shiver, feeling suddenly as if the deathly coldness of the sea had got into her own veins.

"It must have been terrible for you and your parents," she added in a softer voice. "But terrible for Gordon, too. If it was Gordon. It sounds as if he did his best. And you say he was nearly drowned himself."

"*He* said so. I didn't," Neil told her sharply. "And if he was clinging to the dinghy all the time, and was fully prepared to do so when it capsized, he didn't run much risk."

"What do you mean?" said Caroline, looking at him with horror. "Do you really think that he wouldn't even have tried to save a drowning woman, who was his own wife, too?"

"More than that," said Neil grimly. "I'm thinking that he deliberately murdered her. I've thought so ever since it happened."

6

"**N**O!" The denial burst from Caroline with a vehemence that made the motor-cyclist straighten and turn his head towards them.

She had not been entirely unconscious of the darker suspicion Neil could be harbouring, concerning his sister's death, but to hear it put so bluntly into words shook her considerably.

"I can't prove it," Neil went on, as if she hadn't spoken. "He was too cunning for that. He had even paved the way for the crime by telling several of their holiday acquaintances that he was subject to cramp when swimming, and never liked going out of his depth. Being in a foreign country, too, helped him. Nobody really knew them, or the true situation between them. I happened to be touring Spain and

Portugal at the time, with no settled address, and couldn't be reached in time. Nobody but I knew that Rosalind was thinking of leaving Longton. She had kept it dark, partly because she was afraid of upsetting the parents and partly because it was her way to be reticent. There was an enquiry, of course, but there seemed no apparent reason to doubt Longton's statement."

"But it could have been just an accident, and happened exactly as he said," Caroline protested.

"No." Neil's denial was as emphatic as her's had been. "He made one bad mistake. That scarf that was supposed to have been blown overboard. Rosalind hadn't got a scarf."

"Oh, but she must have done," declared Caroline. "Every woman owns at least one."

"Not Rosalind," answered Neil firmly. "If anybody mistakenly gave her one for a present she always thanked them nicely and handed it on to somebody else. She had a horror of scarves ever since she was nearly strangled by one, when she was nine years old. It was a long, dangling thing she had slung round her neck one cold day when she was riding up and down on her bicycle. An end of it caught in her front wheel and very nearly throttled the life out of her. She was rather ashamed of her phobia, though, and very few people knew about it. I'm pretty sure Longton didn't, but he ought to have remembered that she never wore a scarf, when he told his story."

"Perhaps she was trying to get over her fear," Caroline suggested.

"I went to Brittainy later and managed to interview a couple of people who saw the dinghy set off," Neil said, shaking his head. "The man couldn't remember seeing any scarf and the woman was positive that Rosalind was not wearing one. When I faced Longton with this he said she had the thing folded up small in her pocket and got it out to tie over her head. That was when it blew over the side."

"It could have happened like that," Caroline asserted.

"It didn't," said Neil. "I looked into his eyes while he said it, and saw the truth in them for an instant. He was triumphant and afraid and slinking and grinning all at the same time. And as soon as he had got his hands on the money, he vanished, and apparently changed his name and pretended to be a bachelor. Does that look like innocence?"

"Oh God! I don't know what to think!" muttered Caroline.

Then she asked herself guiltily why she was even listening to these accusations against the man she loved. And answered did she really love Gordon? Hadn't she felt secretly for some months now, a dark suspicion that she had been trapped by her own longings into marriage with a superficially charming stranger?

But Neil Fuller was even more of a stranger than her husband.

"Why should I believe you? How do I know you haven't made all this up?" she asked desperately.

"For what reason?" he asked, staring at her in the dim light. Then he turned his head and leaned back with a kind of sigh. "No, I haven't invented it," he said soberly. "Any more than I have the fact that your husband is not working for Dobson and Perks, though he said he was, that you don't really have any idea where he is or what he's doing."

Caroline acknowledged that the point had gone home by a brief silence. Then she said wretchedly: "You hate him, don't you? That's why you've hunted him out and are telling me this horrible story?"

"No, that's not the reason at all," he said quietly.

"Don't you see I can't judge where the truth lies when — when I've only heard your version," she hurried on. "Oh, I don't really doubt that you believe it's the right one, but I have to be sure. I'm the man's wife — if it really is Gordon you're talking about."

"So was Rosalind," said Neil. "And it's the very fact that you are the fellow's wife now that's driven me to try to open your eyes to what he is, a cold, calculating murderer. Don't you realize that you may be in danger?"

"Me? In danger?" exclaimed Caroline faintly. "Oh no!"

The familiar interior of the Fiat, his tall shape beside her, the public house and the couple just going into the Saloon, the motor-cyclist still tinkering with his machine under the light, all seemed suddenly insubstantial and unmeaning.

"I've found out quite a bit about you lately," Neil was saying. "At first I was only interested in you because you were the wife of Longton — Lane, as he calls himself now. I recognized him by chance not long ago and followed him here to Oxridge, but there wasn't time to make many enquiries then. It was easy to find out more, however, when I learned you were a local celebrity, a writer whose books people had actually seen for sale in shop windows and standing on library shelves. They were quite eager to tell me how successful you were and what a pretty penny you must be making."

"They were exaggerating," protested Caroline. "And what has this got to do with — ?"

"They told me the house was yours, too, not Lane's, left to you by a well known Oxridge resident, that nobody knew very much about Lane himself, who was away a lot, but that you were a nice quiet young lady, but a bit on the shy side."

He turned suddenly towards her. "It was then I began to see you as a possible victim," he told her.

"A possible victim?" she repeated, incredulously. But inwardly she was hearing again Mrs. Hedges discoursing on murdered women who were natural born victims because of their blindness and complacency.

"Don't you see the terrible likeness

between your situation and Rosalind's?" muttered Neil.

"No," gasped Caroline.

"Oh, you have two arms," said Neil, with the note of bitterness again. "And you're a bit older than my sister was and ought to be a bit wiser, I suppose. But there's a certain similarity in your characters and you have money of your own, like she did."

"But I earn it. It's income," faltered Caroline.

"Yes, but it won't die with you," Neil pointed out quietly. "Not at once, anyway, and, if your books have a lasting quality and a bit of luck, too, it might even go on coming in for years. The house, too, can't be worth less than ten thousand pounds. And I've no doubt when you married Longton you made a will in his favour."

"He made one in mine, too," said Caroline faintly.

"Of course. It would have seemed odd if he hadn't. But I wonder what he's got to leave. My guess is he's worked through Rosalind's money by now."

Caroline was silent. There seemed a terrible logic in all that this man had said. Her reason accepted it. Her writer's mind, with its bent for plot-making and skill in putting effect to cause and sequence to sequence found it frighteningly convincing. But why wasn't her heart crying out against it? Why wasn't intuition rejecting it? Why couldn't she say that what Neil was telling her couldn't possibly be true because she knew Gordon: knew that he was utterly incapable of the cruelty and callousness and cold, calculating evil ascribed to him?

She continued silent, and Neil began to speak again, quietly and deliberately.

"At first I thought I would let Longton know I'd discovered him, and that this might make him go carefully. That's why I rang up, though some fellow in the pub told me he was still away. When you answered I wondered if telling you what I knew about your husband might protect you. But it wasn't easy to know how to start. I didn't want you simply refusing to listen or even sending for the police. I'm afraid I was pretty indecisive to begin with, but I felt I had to do something and not just go away and let things take their probably nasty course. Then, when I called yesterday morning, you yourself showed me the way to lead you to find out some of the truth when you told me that your husband worked for Dobson and Perks. You see, it was Rosalind who worked for them. She was Dobson's secretary, and he took her back after the accident, though her efficiency must have been diminished, poor girl."

Caroline stared at him. "So that's how — " she began.

"How Longton knew enough about the firm to be able to pretend convincingly," Neil finished for her. "Rosalind left when she married him, but Dobson was at the wedding, and she used to go back and see him from time to time, I know. He wouldn't have recognized my sister's bridegroom of six years ago in the recent snap you showed him of yours, however, not without the beard and after such a brief acquaintance."

"No," murmured Caroline.

She admitted to herself now that she had always found Gordon's business a little mysterious, and his working hours odd. He would make no more that two or three brief visits to London while spending a couple of weeks at home idling, then vanish for another couple of weeks — occasionally less, ostensibly on the firm's affairs.

What had he actually been doing during all those absences?

She started as Neil laid a hand gently on her shoulder and pressed lightly.

"I'm sorry," he said. "If you need help at any time, call on me. I'll let you have my phone number."

He scribbled on a piece of paper and handed it to her. Then he opened the car door and prepared to get out, leaning towards her again to say: "Take my advice in the meantime and change that will. Leave your property to a friend or a lost cause or a cats' home instead of to your husband, and let him know about it as soon as you have done it — but on no account before."

Caroline listened with a kind of wonder. He seemed so much in earnest, so genuinely concerned for her that she could not feel anger. What he was hinting at was so appalling as to be impossible. What ever he said, how could she believe so easily that the man to whom she had given herself meant to murder her in cold blood for the sake of her house and her royalties? That he had married her only for what he could get out of her was hard enough to accept and hateful to her self-love.

"I think you mean to be kind," she told Neil. "But — but I shall have to think about all you've told me. Gordon might have a perfectly good explanation for — for everything."

He sighed, shook his head, muttered

a goodnight and walked to his own car, the tan and cream vehicle she had noticed.

Caroline sat for a few moments, more shaken that she had let him see, then, still in a mental tumult, switched on her engine and turned the Fiat towards home. As she swung onto the road, she heard the motor-bike roar into life and presently saw in the driving-mirror the young man in the crash helmet riding sedately behind her. He passed the entrance of Willow Lodge as she was driving into the garage and she did not see him pull up only a little distance away, turn his machine and coast quietly back.

Caroline had known at once, by the emptiness of the garage, that Gordon had not come home, and the knowledge was a relief to her. Colonel came running round the side of the house to greet her, his tail erect and poker straight. Together they went into the quiet house that seemed to her now to have an air of waiting, like a wood before a storm.

She went into her writing-room, choosing it because it had nothing of Gordon's in it. Here she could be entirely her own woman. She flung her jacket on a chair and sat down at the desk, resting her head on her hands. She had told Neil Fuller that she would think, and that is what she must do.

She believed that he was speaking the truth when he said that Gordon had been married once to his sister, and that she had been drowned while out boating with him off the Breton coast. But she couldn't believe Gordon had murdered her. The evidence of the scarf was too flimsy for words. Only a thoroughly prejudiced man could have built so much on it. Why, Gordon could have given Rosalind the scarf himself and she might not have wanted to disappoint him by telling him she hated the things. She might even have grown out of her curious phobia.

Brothers didn't know everything about their sisters — especially their married sisters.

As for Gordon's silence on the subject of his previous marriage and its tragic ending, that could be explained in psychological terms. He must have suffered a tremendous shock, which could easily have resulted in his avoiding all mention of the cause. A state of trauma they called it, didn't they? It might even account for his change of name.

She shied away from the memory of how Neil had said: "I looked into his eyes and saw the truth in them for an instant. He was triumphant and afraid and slinking and grinning all at the same time," and her own failure to protest at such a picture.

She glanced at her watch. It was not yet ten o'clock. There was still time for her husband to return tonight. The thought roused feelings of dismay in her. How could she carry on as if nothing had happened? Yet, if she truly believed that he was mentally and emotionally disturbed, how could she tax him with having lied to her and deceived her? How could she face him with his cruel past?

And, said a treacherous little voice in her mind, if Neil's fear for her own safety should actually be justified, wouldn't it be wiser to feign ignorance while secretly alert and watchful?

In an effort to appear normal, in case her husband surprised her sitting brooding in the writing-room tonight, she went into the small sitting-room and switched on the television set. But she took in very little of what she saw and heard, and, when midnight came, turned off some fantasy-thriller which seemed hardly more peculiar than her own affairs and went to bed, but not to sleep.

Her thoughts formed a circle of worry. Her head ached, as the questions went round and round. What really happened in that boat? Why hadn't Gordon told her about Rosalind? Was her own explanation the true one? Had Gordon changed his name legally? Or was she really Mrs. Longton, not Mrs. Lane? And what difference did that make? What was his actual occupation? Why had he pretended to be working for Dobson and Perks? What really happened in that boat? Why hadn't Gordon told her? Why? Why? Why?

Feeling hot and feverish, at last she gave up the struggle to compose her mind and sleep. She sat up and switched on the bedside lamp. The old fashioned rosewood furniture gleamed smugly in the big airy room. Gordon's bed, neatly made, waited flat and empty next to her own. The dressing-table glittered with glass and silver. She looked at the tall-boy that had belonged to Aunt Lilian's long dead husband and was now used by Gordon, then threw back the bedclothes and got out of bed.

Throwing on a nylon housecoat, she went across to the handsome piece of furniture and jerked open one drawer after another, standing on a chair to reach the top ones. She knew what she would find in each of them. Handkerchiefs, ties, socks, underclothes, pyjamas, all showing nothing but a laundry mark. There were no surprises. Nothing hidden beneath the obvious.

Then she opened the door of Gordon's wardrobe and looked at the shirts and jackets, the couple of suits, hanging within. Her husband always took his own clothes to the cleaners, so she had never before gone through his pockets. She did so now with a touch of shame, feeling that she was prying, looking for something Gordon wished to keep from her, telling herself her upbringing had made her too nice.

She noticed that he had taken only one suit away with him. A suede car-coat seemed to be the only other object missing from the wardrobe. And in the pockets of the remaining suit a crumpled handkerchief, a loose button, a sixpence, appeared to be all there was to find.

Then, in a pocket of his winter overcoat, she discovered, pressed down into a corner, a rolled up scrap of thick paper. Smoothing it out, she saw that it was a ticket of admittance to the Pier Pavilion Fulhaven.

She frowned, wondering when Gordon could have been there. He and she had never visited the South Coast together at any time, for he had always expressed a dislike of its crowded resorts and turned up his nose at them even out of season. Yet here was evidence that he had visited one of them as recently as last winter or early spring, for he had had this coat cleaned, she remembered, just before Christmas. His so-called business trips had always been, according to him, to the Midlands or Industrial North. This was why, he had said, he never asked her to accompany him.

For a long moment, she stared at the

tell-tale scrap of paper. Then, not quite knowing why, she rolled it up again and pushed it back into the pocket where she had found it.

Now determined to carry through what she had started, Caroline went downstairs to the small sitting-room again, where there was a desk used by her husband to keep papers in and where he did any writing he found necessary — which was very little, she had noticed.

It was unlocked. The papers inside were neatly and methodically placed. Bills, paid and unpaid. Unanswered letters. Advertisements. It struck her, as she went through the letters, how few there were, how strangely impersonal, and how recent. None from anybody who could truly be called a friend. And nothing predated their marriage.

Among the advertisements were some from car dealers which she wondered why Gordon had kept, for they featured expensive cars quite beyond his pocket, she would have thought. They stirred uneasy doubts in her, for a man who was anticipating inheriting a good sum of money might well be tempted by such things. Also, there was a snippet, evidently cut from a newspaper, offering a cottage to let for the holiday season, situated in a quiet and peaceful position near a Cornish cove noted for its dangerous currents.

Strange, surely, that he should fancy such a place after losing his first wife by drowning! Strange, too, that he had never mentioned his interest in it to herself!

She shivered as if suddenly chilly as she replaced what she had found, telling herself that, after all, he might be saving it for a friend.

She was about to shut the desk up again, when she noticed a scrap of paper tucked into one of the pigeon-holes. She pulled it out and found that it was wrapped round a couple of tablets that looked like aspirins. But it was the paper itself that interested

her, for it was part of a used envelope
and showed a portion of the address
that had been written on it. The name
had been torn off. There remained:
' — House, — un Way, Fulhaven,
Kent.'

Fulhaven again, thought Caroline.
Was there any significance in this
find? She decided that there could
be. Any casual visitor, in Fulhaven
for half a day, might buy a ticket
to the Pier Pavilion, but a used
envelope suggested a connection more
permanent. She tried to read the date
mark cancelling the stamp and after
much effort deciphered it. The second
of March of the current year.

She thought back. Yes. At that time
Gordon was in Manchester — or said
he was. Of course, the envelope might
have been addressed to a complete
stranger and have been given to him
simply as a container for the aspirins,
or whatever they were. Only, in that
case, wasn't it odd that the place name
on it should be the same as that on

the ticket she had found? Could it be that Fulhaven was where Gordon was spending the time that was supposed to be occupied by business trips to the Midland and the North?

7

CAROLINE went slowly and thoughtfully upstairs to bed again. She no longer felt ashamed of searching through her husband's belongings. In fact her whole attitude had changed and she felt she could no longer owe trust to somebody who had shown her so little. An active distrust of her husband was not far from her mind, though she tried to keep a negative rather than a positive attitude towards him.

She would not allow herself to believe that Gordon had really murdered his first wife. As for the possibility that he intended to kill her for the sake of inheriting her possessions, the idea still seemed quite fantastic. Yet she could not deny to herself that she had found something sinister in his keeping that advertisement for the Cornish cottage.

She, herself, as her husband knew, was a very poor swimmer, a mere splasher in the shallows. It would not be hard to fake a bathing accident, with her as victim, in that dangerous little cove, if she could be lured out of her depth.

Without warning, a terrible sense of desolation came over her. There, in the quiet house that had been bequeathed to her by a woman who had loved her with a maternal affection, full of the comforts of civilization, she was aware of the loneliness and the vulnerability of every human being; of the jungle that pressed against the stockade built of law and good custom and decency and of the traitors inside the gates who would tear it down if they could. She mourned, not so much for her own lost illusions as to her own blind treachery to something deep within herself.

She put out the light and tried to sleep, though she was sure she never could that night. But unhappiness brought a kind of numbness and eventually she did sleep.

She woke to broad daylight, vaguely comforted by a dream she had had of Aunt Lilian, though she could not remember it clearly.

One thing was clear to her morning mind, however, and that was that it was impossible to carry on with her marriage as if nothing had happened. If Gordon returned today there would have to be a showdown between them. Whatever he had done or not done, no wife could or should accept the way she had been kept in the dark and lied to.

Perhaps if her husband could give her some satisfactory explanation of his behaviour they could come to a new understanding of one another and start again. Perhaps it would be better to make a clean break.

But suppose Gordon did not return today, or tomorrow, or the next day, she thought as she fastened her dressing-gown and thrust her feet into mules. Was she simply to sit at home awaiting his pleasure? Couldn't she do something more active to pass the time?

She could go to Fulhaven. The idea came to her as she stood staring unseeingly at a thrush that was taking brief little runs across the dewy turf, cocking its head to bring one round bright eye to bear on any possible source of worms. The resort was no more than forty miles away and a drive there would be very pleasant on such a fine day.

She might even find out something important. It was a pity the actual name of the house had been torn off that envelope, as well as so much of the road name. But, though Fulhaven was a fair sized place, there could not be many streets called Ways there, and certainly not ones ending in 'un'. She could consult a local directory, perhaps, once she got there.

The part of her that was Carole Bannister, the author, took actual pleasure in the idea of tracking down the house to which the torn envelope had been addressed. She had always enjoyed the research necessary to provide authentic historical settings for her tales. She liked ferreting out odd facts, even if she could make no actual use of them at the time. She took pride in putting together fragments of information to make an interesting whole. The mystery surrounding Gordon would have appealed to her in this way before had it not been for her own personal involvement. Today she felt curiously detached and free.

She could even feel a certain wry amusement at the thought of how much Mrs. Hedges would enjoy the drama of Caroline's disillusionment and the way it had come about, if only she knew of it. As it was there was a look of curiosity in the daily's eyes as she greeted her employer in the kitchen.

"Mr. Lane still not back then?" she said, as she took off her unbecoming hat and rolled it up.

"How did you know?" asked Caroline, who was washing up her breakfast things in the sink and turned now with a sudden absurd suspicion.

"I had a feeling," declared Mrs. Hedges, unrolling her overall. She rather spoilt the effect of this claim to intuitive powers by adding. "I've never known Mr. Lane go without his eggs and bacon of a morning and you're washing up for one."

"No," said Caroline, "he hasn't come home yet."

"And no word neither? Well, don't you worry, Mrs. Lane. I don't suppose nothing's happened to him," said Mrs. Hedges. "A man don't take thought for others same as a woman does. Now if *you'd* said you'd be home on a certain day and there was a hitch of some sort you'd have phoned or sent a telegram. Though Mr. Lane might well have done that and nobody the wiser. Telegrams aren't what they used to be, and that's a fact. When I was a girl there was nothing quicker, barring talking direct. Now it's my belief somebody walks with the things and them boys on the red motor-bikes come dashing up at the last minute just as a bit of eye-wash."

She flung open the back door for Colonel, who was crying to be let in after his early morning walk and sniff-round. The sound of a motor-bike engine came in with the cat.

"Hark!" exclaimed Mrs. Hedges dramatically. "P'raps that's a telegram now."

She held the door open and waited, while the noise increased in volume then receded a little, then she shut it and reentered the kitchen, where the cat was already finishing off the remains of his breakfast he had purposely left for this occasion.

"It's gone past," she said regretfully.

"It seems to have stopped," remarked Caroline, who had continued to listen with some interest. "I think somebody up the road must own a motor-bike."

"I don't know who it can be then, Mrs. Lane." declared Mrs. Hedges, who knew a great deal about the local residents. "Mr. Ball is too old and the Dawsons have only got daughters, though you do get girls riding them things sometimes."

"This is a man," said Caroline. "I've seen him about lately."

"The Wellses have got a car and no kids," mused Mrs. Hedges, rolling up her sleeves. "And Sir George Neville is too posh. Somebody's dating one of them Dawson girls I expect."

"He always seems to be alone, and he spent a good deal of time at the Hand in Hand last night," Caroline told her, shaking her head.

Mrs. Hedges paused on her way to the broom cupboard to give her employer a sharp look.

"Had a bit of an evening out, I suppose," and it was clear she was thinking of Caroline and not of the young man with the motor-bike. "Oh well, it's better than sitting moping at home. Are you feeling better this morning, Mrs. Lane? I must say you don't look quite so peaky, if I may say so."

"Yes, I'm better thank you," said Caroline, turning back to the sink, and finishing her task there while her henchwoman rummaged in the cupboard. When she saw Emma's broad behind emerging, she added: "But I'm thinking of taking a little trip to the coast. I may even stay away a few days. So do you think you could come in morning and evening, over the weekend, to feed Colonel and give him a little petting?"

Mrs. Hedges turned round quickly, dropping a tin of polish and hitting herself over the shins with the mop.

"The weekend?" she repeated, her pale eyes open wide and her small mouth a little open too.

"Yes," said Caroline. "I don't want to impose on your good nature, but if you could look after Colonel for me I should be very grateful. And of course I shall pay you for the extra time."

"Yes," said Mrs. Hedges slowly, as

if consulting an invisible engagement book. "I think I can do that for you, Mrs. Lane. We can't have His Nibs neglected."

She stooped ponderously and recovered the polish, which Colonel had been cautiously eyeing from a distance.

"Mr. Lane — " she said and stopped.

"May come home in the meanwhile," Caroline finished for her composedly. "In that case there won't be any need for you to bother. I shall leave a note explaining." She added abruptly: "No. Come in night and morning in any case, please."

"Certainly," said Mrs. Hedges, straightening herself and fixing speculative eyes on Caroline's face.

But Caroline's face could look almost as inscrutable as the popular Western idea of the slant eyed mask-like countenance of a highborn Chinese lady, and Emma began to show signs of bafflement. She was obviously wondering what had cropped up since yesterday morning to cause this sudden decision. Had it anything to do with the red-headed visitor? Or the brief visit to London? Whatever it was all about, it couldn't be what she'd thought. You didn't go to the coast to see a doctor.

"Will you be starting this morning?" she asked.

"As soon as I've packed a few things," said Caroline. "Thank you very much, Mrs. Hedges. I knew I could rely on you."

She hurried upstairs, feeling rather pleased with herself. At first she had intended to go to Fulhaven just for the day, but it had suddenly occurred to her that there might be advantages in prolonging the visit. It would give her more time to look around and she would have a chance to be quite on her own for a little while, without the danger of Gordon appearing at any moment and facing her with the crisis she knew must come but couldn't help dreading.

She thought about the impulse that had made her ask Mrs. Hedges to come and look after Colonel whether her husband returned during her absence or not. Did she distrust him so much that she would not now leave the cat she knew he tolerated rather than liked, to his care? Or did she simply desire to be completely independent of him now?

A little of both, she decided as she packed a trouser-suit and a couple of dresses, underclothes, toilet bag, shoes and night-wear, into a medium-sized case.

The note she must leave for her husband gave her some thought, too. Finally, she made it very brief. "Dear Gordon, Gone away for a few days to get some local colour. Love, Caroline."

Her usually tender conscience did not reproach her for the white lie, under the circumstances. Gordon had too much to answer for himself, when it came to deceitfulness.

She put on a dark green crimplene

suit with a sand coloured blouse and accessories, an outfit she would probably live in for the next few days, she thought, in spite of the things she had packed.

Mrs. Hedges, with Colonel in attendance, saw her off, as she drove away in the mellow sunshine, and there was still that look of speculation in Emma's eyes.

There was no traffic in the lane, but by the time Caroline had reached the main road a motor-cyclist had come roaring up behind her. For a moment she thought it must be the same man who had been at the Hand in Hand the night before and whom Mrs. Hedges had decided must be courting one of the Dawson girls while she was sure he was not. It was then she had a sudden remembrance of the figure with the abnormally large head she had fancied she had seen among the willows. Could it have been a man wearing a crash helmet? Of course! It *was* a man wearing a crash helmet. But what on earth had he been dodging among the trees like that for? Perhaps he was afraid of being accused of trespassing. Had been attracted by the stream no doubt. It did fascinate people, running water, though usually it was small boys who succumbed to the spell. He couldn't really have been spying on her. Or could he?

She thought uneasily of the way the motor-cyclist had hung about while she talked with Neil in the car and had driven after her up the road. Had there really been something wrong with his machine? Or had he just been taking an unusual interest in her?

She peered into her mirror at the man on the machine behind her. He was wearing sunglasses and a black beret. A black scarf covered the lower part of his face. No, it probably wasn't the same man. It was silly to feel so relieved, for, after all, what could anybody gain by following her about? Unless — unless Gordon had secretly decided he wanted a divorce, and was employing an agent to look for evidence upon which he could act.

But that idea was absurd. What possible grounds for suspicion could he have had?

And then it occurred to her that there was a person who might have a reason for putting a spy on her. Neil Fuller. If, that was to say, he didn't believe her when she said she had no knowledge of Gordon's whereabouts, and if he was determined to catch up with his one time brother-in-law.

No, she was imagining things. It wasn't the same motor-cyclist.

He was still behind her when she had left the shops and the parked cars behind and had increased her speed to a pleasant fifty along the tree-lined road that led south to the coast. Well, why shouldn't he be? It was Friday, and others beside herself, might want to take advantage of the promise of a fine weekend at Summer's end and spend it by the sea. There was a car with a pram on top that had also been close behind her from the time she had turned into the High Street, for instance.

Nevertheless, she decided to make a test. On a wider stretch of road she gradually decreased her speed and allowed the car with the pram on top to overtake. Now the motor-cyclist was nearer. *Was* it the same man? Impossible to say. Humped over the handlebars even his height was in doubt, and of his features only nondescript eyebrows and a nose were visible.

She slowed down some more. This was the test. If he passed she would decide he was no more than an uninvolved stranger taking the same road as herself by chance. But if he deliberately hung behind then she might feel she had reasonable grounds for her uneasiness and suspicion. There was a roar heard above the sound of her own engine, and the motor-cyclist had passed and was overtaking the car in front, too.

She relaxed. It was all right. But

it showed what a state her nerves were in to have even considered the possibility that she was being followed. The revelations of the last few days had done this to her.

As she drove on, she allowed her mind to dwell more and more on those revelations, while automatically, she responded to the needs of her task.

Were there more discoveries to come? Would she make any as a result of this trip, or was she on a wild goose chase? After all, the address on that envelope might be totally irrelevant, and she only had half of it in any case. But at least this was an escape from indecision and a mere sitting down and weeping.

Gradually the sunshine and blue sky, and the charm of the route she was taking through the rich Garden of England, lifted her spirits until she could imagine her cares and problems actually left behind at Willow Lodge. She determined to make this a brief holiday and nothing more.

She passed hop-gardens where many of the vines had been stripped down, leaving only skeletal supports, and others that were hanging veils of leaf and fruit in lovely green. The fruit had long been taken from the cherry-trees, but in the apple orchards there were avenues after avenues of trees with branches bowed down with ripening globes and fallen apples lying in the bright green grass below, hovered over by butterflies and pecked at by birds.

Hand-written notices tempted the motorist to stop, as they advertised Coxes at ninepence and a shilling a pound and windfalls as cheap as three-pence.

Caroline pulled up at one gate displaying such a sign, where an old house stood a little way back from the road, embowered in orchards. A motor-bike was parked at the verge and a head wearing a black beret bobbed up on the other side of the hedge as she drew to a halt. But she had dismissed the notion that she was being followed and did not allow herself to be diverted from her purpose, which was to quench a growing thirst with some juicy apples.

It had grown warm as the morning advanced, and as she stepped out of the car she felt the sunshine fall upon her thin clad shoulders with real power, for she had taken off her jacket.

There was a garden table just inside the gate, with an old man behind it; a clean and rosy old man in his shirtsleeves, weighing a scoop full of clean rosy apples taken from a deep basket at his side. He waved away a wasp with a fearless gesture, as Caroline entered a garden where stocks, dahlias, asters and nasturtiums rioted untidily, and tipped the apples into a large paperbag. This he handed across the table to the motor-cyclist, who was standing with his back towards the gate. A coin changed hands the reverse way, and the customer turned away.

It was as she came face to face with him that Caroline felt a pang of uneasiness again. Surely he was very like the man at the Hand in Hand last night, though the dark glasses still hid the eyes.

But he stumped past her in his heavy boots with his face averted, as if he was admiring the flowers, and the old man was smiling politely, anticipating an order, so there was nothing she could do to confirm or deny her suspicion.

The apple-seller served her in the leisurely way that went well with his serene old age and the garden and the sunshine and talked contentedly of the fine day and the abundant harvest in a voice that was as Kentish as the fruit.

Caroline felt that she must not hurry him, but while she responded politely to his remarks, she listened for the motor-cyclist to start up his machine, If he drove away at once, she thought, then she would know she was being unnecessarily suspicious again. But if he lingered —

When she reached the gate with her apples, he was storing his own bag of

fruit in his carrier-bag with one hand
while he held a well bitten Worcester
in the other. A trickle of juice was
running down his chin, now free of
the black scarf.

Caroline smiled at him deliberately,
and in response he gave her a smile that
was strangled practically at birth and
turned away his head. It was the sight
of the crash helmet tucked inside the
carrier bag that had made her decide
to approach him with some sort of
challenge.

"I say," she said boldly. "Haven't I
seen you before?"

He finished fastening the bag, took
out a handkerchief and wiped his chin.
Then he said gruffly: "What d'you
mean? Seen me before?"

"Yes. Weren't you in the Hand
in Hand at Oxridge last night," said
Caroline

He shook his head, his face wooden.
She wished she could read the eyes
behind those dark glasses.

"Never touch the stuff," he declared

and took a decisive bite at the apple in his hand.

"Oh. Sorry," Caroline said. "It must be that you were following me up earlier this morning."

He said nothing to that, apparently staring after a car that had just passed.

She got back into the Fiat and wound down the window, watching, though not overtly, while he took his place astride his machine and seemed prepared to enjoy the rest of his apple in that position.

If that was simply delaying tactics two could play at it, she thought. And whatever the man had said she was not convinced he was the innocent he made out to be.

She took a large ripe apple and bit into it thoughtfully. It would take several minutes to finish it up, if she was sufficiently leisurely about it, while the motor-cyclist was practically down to the core of his own fruit. He should be ready to ride off at any moment.

Almost at once he disposed of this core in a messy and untidy manner by tossing it under the old man's hedge. Then he drew another apple from a pocket of his jacket and began to munch steadily again.

He was still at it when Caroline had taken the final bite of her own Cox's and she wondered whether to start on a second fruit. But she had a mental picture of the two of them sitting there grimly eating through a large supply of apples simply to foil each other, and was seized with a desire to laugh. It was difficult to take the situation seriously after that. And she was not at all sure that she was not making a fool of herself, anyway. The crash helmet in the saddle-bag probably meant nothing. Most motor-cyclists must carry them.

With a mental shrug, she poked her apple-core into the nearest ash-tray and started up the engine.

The young man on the motor-bike turned his sunglasses briefly on her as she drove past him and went on eating. A temporary increase in traffic diverted her attention, then a delivery van coming up behind her hid him entirely from view.

8

CAROLINE drove down the hill to the harbour at Fulhaven, between the terraces of tall Victorian houses, at precisely twelve o'clock. She had taken longer than she had anticipated, owing to a spate of big vans and lorries on the road, which had held up the lighter traffic with its cumbersome pace. One or two motor-bikes had passed her on the way, weaving in between cars and heavy vehicles and getting easily ahead. Several times she had caught sight of a machine keeping steadily along two or three places behind her. But the rider was bare-headed and goggled and had a pillion passenger, a girl with long fair hair whipping back from her face. So this could not be 'her' motor-cyclist, Caroline decided.

When she reached the sea she saw

that the tide was partly in. The harbour was crowded with cabin-cruisers, small motor-boats and sailing dinghies, with a few workman-like fishing vessels to show that the place was not entirely given up to pleasure craft. Most of the boats shone with bright paint and glossy varnish, which were made doubly effective by being reflected in the water. Beyond the curving harbour wall, with its little stone jetty and white-washed lighthouse, white tipped waves danced on the sparkling blue sea.

Caroline left her car at the kerb and got out to join the brown contented looking loafers at the railings and to stare placidly with them for a while. Black-headed gulls perched on masts and circled overhead. Herring-gulls lay easily on the wind, turning their heads from side to side and uttering their mewing cries. The air was deliciously fresh, with a faint salt tang to it and a hint of the seaweed that had marked the wall below her with a green signature.

The scene was a novel one to her, for she had not visited Fulhaven since her childhood and had forgotten what the place looked like. No doubt there had been some alterations, she thought, and turned to gaze about her in a landward direction. In front of her, on the other side of the road, was a triangle of short green turf with a wooden seat occupied by a couple of aged characters. A telephone-box stood at one apex, and close to it was a board displaying the times of the tides and what appeared to be a map of the town. Another road lay on the other side of this oasis, lined with shops, the Harbour Hotel, a small restaurant and a humble public house that looked as if it would be a haunt of fisher-folk.

It was the map of the town that interested Caroline most. She forgot her intention to regard this trip as no more than a holiday. Detective zeal possessed her again. She crossed the road eagerly and examined the map, seeking for a road marked on it with

162

a name that ended with 'un Way.' But there seemed to be no such road.

Very carefully, inch by inch, she examined the map again. She found four Ways, but none ended with the syllable she had seen on the envelope. She traced one of these with a finger. It was a long road and changed its name half way, starting as Down Way and finishing Down Road. It began quite close to the sea.

Then she felt a small thrill as it suddenly occured to her that the letter she had taken for a 'u' in the handwriting on the envelope might just as easily have been half a 'w', for it had been right at the edge of the paper, where it was torn across.

Feeling as elated now as when some small piece of information had fallen into place during one of her spells of historical research, she mentally marked the exact position of Down Way in relation to where she was, then turned to go back to the car.

As she watched for coming traffic

before crossing the road, she found herself looking straight into the telephone-box and gave a start of surprise. Peering through the glass at her was a face. Without goggles or sunglasses she recognised it definitely at last as the face of the motor-cyclist in the Hand in Hand.

Then it was replaced by the back of a dark head as the man in the box turned sharply. But Caroline knew she had not been mistaken. She looked for the motor-bike and found it on the other side of the green island. Instinctively she pretended to have noticed nothing, and was about to cross the road when a long-haired blonde in stained and hideous jeans and a man's suede jacket went and tapped on the glass door of the telephone-kiosk.

"It's okay," she called shrilly. "I found my friends. Thanks again for the lift." And with a gay little wave, passed on.

So that was it! The apple-eater had merely taken off his beret and changed his sunglasses for goggles and had followed her just sufficiently far behind to be out of her sight part of the time. And the pillion-passenger that had still further confused her had been no more than a hitch-hiker whom he had picked up on the way.

She remembered now a group of them standing with their thumbs up by the side of the road. Tousle-headed, bearded youths and lank haired girls, dressed in a weird collection of untidy garments and all hung round with duffle-bags and guitars.

She had shaken her head firmly at them and driven on. They might have been inoffensive enough, of course. On the other hand they might prove a menace to a solitary woman. And she didn't like cadging, anyway, and had never cadged herself, even when she was as young as they were and probably poorer.

The question now was had she been followed deliberately, or was it sheer coincidence? The reaction of the young man in the telephone-box had looked like guilt. So had his answer to her by the apple orchard. On the other hand, it could have been embarrassment each time. Perhaps he had been afraid she was trying to claim acquaintance with him for her own amorous ends. Though he hadn't hesitated to befriend the long haired blonde. More to his taste, perhaps, than her thirty-four year old self. Well, that was reasonable, after all. He didn't look more than twenty-two or three himself.

Smiling inwardly a little wryly, but puzzled and uneasy, too, she crossed to her car and got in. She kept an eye unobtrusively on the telephone-box as she restarted the engine. The man was still inside.

The road climbed up to the Promenade, where more green turf and flower-beds lay on one side, ending in railings and a drop to the sparkling sea. On the other side were solid looking hotels and well kept guesthouses. Caroline could not see the motor-cyclist following, but much of her attention was given to finding her way, while watching the road for parked cars which suddenly moved out into the traffic, excited dogs, dreamy old men, children sucking lollies and indifferent to all else, women stopping to peer into beachbags.

She drove past the turning she wanted, seeing the name-plate, 'Down Way', just too late. Rather than reverse the car, she pulled in to the verge and stopped. There were other cars parked ahead and no yellow lines or other restricting signs, so she got out, locked the door and decided to explore on foot.

It was a pleasing looking road with good hotels at each corner and a strip of garden down the middle. There were more hotels beyond, but these got smaller as Caroline proceeded. She was glad of this, for it was easier to take note of the buildings on both sides of the road. Her heart gave a little jump when she came upon the first guesthouse. Inevitably it was named 'Sea View', though the guests staying there could have only a squinting glimpse of the sea from its windows in front. Then she came upon 'Cliff House' and felt another stir of excitement. Could this be the address she was seeking? But on the other side of the road stood 'Haven House' and next to it 'Ocean House'.

She stood still for a moment in dismay and disappointment, realizing what a hopeless task she had set herself after all. Three names ending in 'House' already, and the road stretched for some way yet, and bent round in a curve that hid its full extent from her, though perhaps it became Down Road beyond the bend.

The farther she had walked along this side road the fewer people she had met, though here, too, there was an occasional parked car. It was a time of day of least activity, and she had caught glimpses through windows of hotel guests seated at gleaming white tables and even sniffed some savoury odours wafting up from basement kitchens.

She wondered now whether to give up the search and go and have lunch somewhere herself. It was then that she noticed, about a hundred yards ahead, a man in casual clothes coming down some stone steps leading from the porch of a house with a great blue flowering hydrangea beside it. His face was turned from her, but the sun shone on his fair hair, and his shape and his walk were entirely familiar to her. For a moment her heart seemed to stop, then began beating much too fast. It was Gordon, her husband. She had no doubt of it. Yet she was amazed, too.

Without looking left or right, he got into the car drawn up at the kerb — his own Vauxhall, she saw now.

Three woman, walking abreast and chattering brightly, passed her and temporaily obstructed her view. She heard a car engine start up and a vehicle drive away. By the time the women had turned into a gateway and ceased to block her vision, the car had gone round the bend. And there was only the sound of it receding into the distance.

It had happened so quickly that Caroline continued to stand on the pavement as if unable to move. Now she walked forward, but slowly, bewildered by the suddenness with which her seemingly hopeless task had been accomplished. She had no idea what to do next.

Outside the gateway through which she had seen Gordon emerge she stopped. There was the magnificent hydrangea with its great blue flowers. She stared up at the house. It was stone coloured, with three floors and a semi-basement. Net curtains at all the windows gave an air of bland secretiveness. In gothic letters on the fanlight over the front door was the name, 'Regency House', and inside the porch, with its stone pillars, she saw a small white plaque. She knew what this was, having seen similar objects outside other guesthouses she had passed. It signified that the place had been given the approval of some local association of caterers and hoteliers.

There was a slight stirring of the net at one of the downstair windows. With sudden decision she pushed open the gate, walked up the path and ascended the stone steps. She was horribly nervous, but she told herself there was nothing unusual about a stranger making enquiries about a friend at a boarding-house at a holiday resort. Whatever she felt inwardly, she must try to appear at ease.

The woman who opened the door in answer to her ring was so calm and placid looking that Caroline felt her own troubled excitement begin to die down at the mere sight of her. She was tall and blonde and big breasted, with a milk white skin, heavy lidded eyes and a voluptuous mouth and throat. A Juno come down from Olympia in a modern, low cut dress and dangling pearl beads, who looked at the caller with a kind of benevolent disinterest.

"Good morning," said Caroline, and

171

swallowed an invisible lump. "I think you have a friend of mine staying here. Mr. Lane. Mr. Gordon Lane."

"No," said the woman. "We have nobody of that name staying, I'm afraid." Her voice was deep and drowsy sounding.

"Oh," said Caroline, confused. "Then — then perhaps he isn't actually staying here. Perhaps he just made enquiries about staying." She wondered whether to say bluntly that she had seen him leaving only a minute ago. But it might seem odd that she had not stopped him and put her questions to him personally.

"I don't know any Mr. Lane at all," said the woman. "I'm sorry. Are you sure you have the right guesthouse? This is Regency House, and I'm Mrs. Lessing."

"Yes, it's the right house," said Caroline. "But — but perhaps my friend hasn't arrived yet." She was thinking fast now. If she could get inside the place, couldn't she manage to examine the register? If Gordon was using a false name it was most likely to be Longton.

"He hasn't booked at all," said Mrs. Lessing. "But I'm not full up. It's the end of the season, you see."

"Then could you let me have a room and board for a day or two, please?" asked Caroline. "My case is in my car, parked round the corner by the Promenade," she explained.

"Yes, I could let you have a double-room," answered Mrs. Lessing serenely. "Then your friend can have the only vacant single one when he comes. I don't serve luncheon. Only breakfast and dinner. That's at seven. I prefer breakfast to be finished serving by nine o'clock. We've no garage, I'm afraid, but there's a car-park about a quarter of a mile away, or you could leave your car where it is. It's allowed, providing you move it once in the twenty-four hours."

While she was talking she was leading Caroline across a thickly carpeted hall with a barometer on one wall and a gilt framed mirror on the other, up a staircase with highly varnished bannisters where their footsteps were equally soundless. When she ceased it was very quiet. Caroline heard the slow, lazy ticking of the grandfather clock on the landing.

The room into which she was shown was clean and tastefully decorated, though the big bed took up a great deal of the space and there was no very interesting view from its one window, as this looked onto the side premises of the house next door. She declared it to be satisfactory, however, agreed to the landlady's casually stated terms and accepted a key.

"I must remember to sign your register," she remarked, as they descended to the ground floor again, and she noticed the ledger lying on the small oak table at the foot of the stairs, together with time-tables and notices of local events. "My name is — Bannister, by the way," she added. "Mrs. Bannister."

She felt herself go hot. She had so nearly said 'Lane,' but remembered just in time that she had described the Mr. Lane she had enquired about as merely a friend.

"No hurry, Mrs. Bannister," said Mrs. Lessing.

"I'll do it when I come back with my case," Caroline promised herself, hoping that then she could examine the ledger without the landlady's presence.

She could see no sign of the motor-cyclist or his machine along by the Promenade, or, indeed, anywhere in sight. But that wasn't to say he had gone. He might very well be observing her from one of the glassed in shelters, or from a seat in the shrubbery, she decided, as she took her case from the Fiat and went back to Regency House.

There was nobody to watch her, however, as she opened the ledger in the hall and examined the entries. Her fellow guests were a family named Cobb, two spinsters, and two single men, Dawson and Tooley, all of whom had arrived the previous Saturday. She looked back to the previous Wednesday, the day Gordon had left Willow Lodge. But nobody had arrived on this date, according to the book, and there was no Longton on that page or on a dozen of the previous ones. Of course, there was often laxness in these matters, she knew. And Gordon might well be calling himself Dawson, though not, she decided, Tooley. It was not, somehow, the sort of name one would choose for oneself.

She signed her pen-name, Carole Bannister, after the last entry, and added the address of her agent in London.

9

A STIFF breeze was blowing, when Caroline came out of one of the hotels along the front that catered for non-residents. She had eaten a three-course luncheon with determination rather than relish, and now had to get through the rest of the day until dinner-time, when presumably all Mrs. Lessing's guests assembled in the dining-room at Regency House.

There were more people about in spite of the wind, but they were walking briskly or sitting in the shelters and on the more protected seats. The deckchairs that dotted the grass between the hotels and the cliff-edge were empty and their striped canvas fluttered stiffly. The flowers in the rose garden that stretched in front of the Grand hotel and the Majestic nodded and dipped and strewed their petals on the neatly hoed earth.

Down below, on the pebbly beach, people had erected wind screens or were sitting behind break-waters. But the sun still shone brightly and white horses tossed their manes on a blue sea that continued to sparkle. A sailing dinghy with red sails swooped and curtseyed out there and gulls were blown about the sky like pieces of white paper.

Caroline fastened her jacket and tied a scarf over her head, thinking as she did so of Rosalind, then instantly trying to banish the thought. The sea drew her, and she walked slowly down a flight of steps that led to the Marine Parade and the beach, then trod uncomfortably over the heaped stones till she reached the finer shingle and sauntered at the tides edge.

Her scarf fluttered about her head and blown spray stung her face. Occasionally she had to take quick evasive action to dodge a breaking wave. It was all very exhilerating and she would have enjoyed it if she had merely been on a holiday visit. But anxiety and suspicion and doubt gnawed at her mind.

After a while she trudged back up the beach, raising her eyes to the clifftop where the heads and shoulders of promenaders were visible and here and there a full length figure leaning over the railings and gazing out to sea. Suddenly she gave a faint cry that the wind snatched away and lost, as she saw that one of these figures was tall and red headed. For a moment she was convinced it was Neil Fuller. She even shouted his name and waved an arm above her head.

There was no response from the man high up on the cliff, and before she could call again he had drawn back and disappeared from her view.

For a few minutes she stood and watched the flight of steps that led down to the Marine parade, half expecting to see him descending them. But only a fat woman in trousers and a head-band came down them, followed by a small man carrying a hold-all.

What a fool she was, thought Caroline, turning away and sitting down in the shelter of a break-water. Of course it couldn't have been Neil. It would have been too much of a coincidence if they had both come down to Fulhaven today. She was hit by a disturbing thought. Unless he had come in search of Gordon, too. But how would he know that Gordon might be here? No, it couldn't have been Neil.

Having decided this, Caroline made a hollow for herself among the grey and golden and amber coloured pebbles and reclined there, hidden from the wind and in the full benison of the sun. She had popped a paper-back into her capacious handbag, and now she took it out and tried to read a little, dividing her attention between the book and a staring small girl and her incurious brother, who had continued his collecting of mysteriously selected stones without taking any notice of the behaviour of an unknown adult.

In spite of herself, she began to relax, The warmth on her eyelids, the rhythmic beating of the waves, the knowledge that she had nothing to do and could make no decision for several hours yet, lulled her into a fatalistic calm. She let her head drop back and closed her eyes. The waves broke with muted thunder, the pebbles hissed as they were drawn back. Thunder and hiss, thunder and hiss, thunder and hiss.

"I say, I'm afraid you'll get wet if you don't move."

Caroline opened her eyes with a start and saw the father of the two children gazing down at her with a friendly grin, while his wife gathered up the family belongings and moved them higher up the beach. The thunder and hiss were certainly nearer now and, sitting up, Caroline saw that the waves were breaking only a couple of yards away. She had slept for nearly an hour and a half.

She was stiff and slightly bemused and she shivered a little in the wind, when she had scrambled onto the Marine Parade and began to walk along it, seeing a sign that read: 'Smugglers' Nook ¾ ml. Afternoon Tea. Morning Coffee. Snacks.'

She was throughly awake by the time she had rounded a small headland, with almost a gale blowing in her face, and found the little house tucked under the cliff and looking over a hedge of bent tamarisk. A gull was perched on the summit of the sloping roof, its plumage ruffled wildly, till it was blown off, uttering a fiercely protesting cry, as she approached.

She made a pot of tea last as long as possible, glad of protection from the mounting wind, but enjoying, in her immunity, the sight of the waves battering the beach and the anchored boats bobbing frantically about near the shore. The place was nearly full, and she was congratulating herself on having a small table to herself in the window, as a group of people paused outside before coming up the steps to the entrance. But a solitary walker, moving with purposeful strides, reached it before them, and the sight of him jolted Caroline out of her temporary complacency. This time there could be no doubt about it. It was Neil Fuller.

Less unprepared now, she did not call his attention to herself. On the contrary, she drew back as his glance went vaguely to the window, for the disturbing thought that had come to her earlier now returned more forcefully. It was too much of a coincidence, their both being here like this! And she found it frightening.

Had Neil tracked her to Fulhaven? Or was the motorcyclist in his employment? If the latter, would there have been time for Neil to have got the message and come down? Had she been mistaken in thinking she had seen him on the cliff-top? She might well have been so, for he had been in her mind, together with Gordon for most of the day.

She lowered her head, pretending to search in her handbag, glad that her back was towards the door as she heard him enter. But she had overlooked the fact that there was a vacant place at her table and that the room was nearly full. She felt rather than saw him standing beside her.

"May I?" he said. Then, as she raised her eyes reluctantly to his, added: "I thought it was you, though I couldn't quite believe it at first."

But he did not look very surprised, she noticed. Was he thinking the same thing about her?

"Hallo," she said. "How — how strange that we should meet here!"

"Yes. Do you often come to Fulhaven?" he said politely, picking up a menu with an unlikely looking smuggler's head on it.

"Not often," Caroline answered. "But it was such a lovely day for a drive, and the idea of the sea — "

"Exactly how I felt," said Neil, poker-faced. "So I took the afternoon off, in case the weather changed tomorrow. Have you had tea? I see you have. What a pity. I was hoping you would have some with me."

"Thank you, but I've had sufficient," replied Caroline with equal politeness, and asked the waitress for her bill, as the girl came to take Neil's order.

When she had paid it she began fastening her jacket and tying on her head-scarf in preparation for her departure.

"Wait a minute," he said in a low voice. "I'd like to talk to you, but I suppose there's no chance here. Have you seen your husband?"

It took her a moment to decide what to answer. Then she shook her head. "Gordon hasn't come home," she said. "I had to get away and think. That's why — " She stared out of window at the sea.

"I see. Are you down just for the day? Or putting up somewhere? Can you have dinner with me tonight?"

Again she shook her head without looking at him. "I'm sorry, but I have to get back," she told him. She didn't have to tell him where 'back' was, she thought. She ventured to look at him. "And you?" she asked.

"It depends," he answered with a slight frown replacing an expression of sharp enquiry he had been directing at her averted face.

He rose courteously as she stood up.

"Goodbye," she said, with a stiff little smile.

As she walked back the way she had come, with the wind behind her now, blowing her skirts against her legs, she had a pang of regret that she had not been able to confide in him. But how could she possibly trust him now? Whatever motive he had in coming here to Fulhaven, to tell him about Regency House would be to deliver Gordon up to him. She couldn't do it. After all, even such a marriage as hers seemed to have become carried obligations with it.

There was a possibility, however, that Neil didn't need to be told, that he knew exactly where to find his enemy. And if so, what did he intend to do about it? Was he really thinking of exacting a belated payment for his sister's death? By exposing him, or by some sort of violent attack?

The thought made her turn and look anxiously behind her, in case Neil had skippped tea and was stealthily following her. But there was no sign of him along the path, and the tide had come so far up the beach now that the spray from the breaking waves was wetting the concrete a little.

As the dinner hour approached, Caroline felt not only an increasing apprehension but a growing determination. She intended to surprise Gordon in whatever guise he was masquerading and demand an explanation of his extraordinary behaviour. But when she drew near Regency House and

187

saw that her husband's car was not outside, she found herself hoping he had not yet arrived, that the moment of truth might be postponed for just a little while longer. After all, there was still nearly an hour and a half to go till dinner time.

She was glad she had left her own car some little distance away, for if Neil saw it and recognized it, there was not much it would tell him as to her actual whereabouts. And the same thing applied to the motor-cyclist. She had seen no more of him, however. Was that because his employer had taken over? Or had she merely been imagining things where he was concerned? There was nothing really impossible in two separate people being in the Hand in Hand at Oxridge one evening and going to a popular resort like Fulhaven at practically the same time the next morning all quite by chance.

But she couldn't believe it applied in this case.

"Too many coincidences!" she told

herself again, as she hung her suit in the wardrobe.

She filled in the time of waiting by taking a bath and dressing in a leisurely manner, putting on one of the two frocks she had brought with her. It was gold in colour, with touches of warm brown that brought deeper colour into her hazel-eyes. Nervousness had made her extra pale, but she lipsticked her mouth till it glowed softly, and brushed her dark hair until it shone. The result gave her a little confidence.

She waited deliberately after the gong had sounded, to give the other guests time to assemble in the dining-room, for she had changed her first plan, which was to wait outside the door as they entered and stop her husband on the threshold. She wanted to avoid a scene, and had decided that she would simply go up to Gordon, as he sat at table, and say hullo as if it was the most unsurprising thing in the world to find him there. Explanations could come afterwards.

She tried to control the feverish pulsing of her blood, as she went downstairs after a sufficient lapse of time. She hesitated for a brief moment, with her hand on the knob of the dining-room door, her heart seeming to reach a climax of violent beating. Then she took a deep breath and entered.

It was a terrible anticlimax to find that Gordon was not there. But there were two tables, still, with nobody at them. Each was laid for one person. One must be meant for her. And the other must be her husband's. She had come down too soon after all.

A thin girl with a sallow skin and heavy black hair was serving soup to a party of four. The Cobbs, no doubt. She looked round as Caroline took her place at the single table bearing her room number, and so did most of the other people in the room, giving polite nods and smiles and murmured goodevenings.

As she acknowledged these, too nervous to be shy about it, she waited tensely for the door to open and the last guest to enter, giving a curt reply to the maid's request to know whether she would take soup or fruit juice to start her meal.

"The doctor's late," remarked one of two oldish young men at a Table for two, (Dawson and Tooley?) to two youngish old women at another. (Miss Masters and Miss Benson).

"He's privileged." answered the one addressed, with a tolerant smile.

Doctor? Surely Gordon wasn't posing as a medical man, now, thought Caroline. That could be criminal. She crumbled a piece of bread into her plate, and stared unseeingly at four michaelmas daisies in a tiny vase on the table.

At last the door opened and a man entered. At sight of him Caroline suddenly found herself completely calm. With quiet self-assurance he walked to the vacant table, a lean, wiry, very clean elderly man with shrewd eyes and a mouth with a little twist to it that was half humorous and half bitter. He lifted a hand in a kind of general salute, as the other guests greeted him.

Now everybody was here. And no Gordon among them. So much was clear. There was to be no deliberately undramatic confrontation with a deceiving husband after all. If he had ever been staying here at all then he had probably left this morning, when she had seen him. At this very moment, she wouldn't mind betting, he was eating cold meat and salad at Willow Lodge and wondering where on earth she had got to.

Well, let him wonder, thought Caroline, beginning on her soup. But what was she to do now? Tackle Mrs. Lessing about her recent guests? There was the problem of what Gordon had been calling himself. How could she possibly explain the situation to a stranger? Or even to a friend, for that matter. It was all so complex and odd.

She ate her way through a very ordinary dinner with her thoughts far away from food. The pink-shaded lights were switched on and remarks were made about the nights 'drawing in' and the weather. One of the women at the next table was inclined to be friendly and made one or two remarks to Caroline, leaning across at the end of the meal to say: "Coffee is served in the lounge. Maria doesn't always remember to tell newcomers. She's Italian and hasn't been here long."

"Thank you," said Caroline, rising with this new acquaintance, seeing an oportunity of getting some information.

"Have you been staying here long?" she asked, as they walked to the door.

"Not quite a week," answered the woman, a plump good-natured looking type, wearing a lot of rings on little fat hands. "Miss Benson and I came last Saturday. Are you staying long?"

"Only a few days, at the most," answered Caroline. "Mrs. Lessing seems to have plenty of vacancies, doesn't she. But I believe one guest left this morning."

"No," said the woman who was obviously Miss Masters, looking surprised. "Nobody has left since Sunday." She smiled. "Nobody has arrived either, except yourself." She lowered her voice. "I believe Dr Hardwick is a permanent guest here."

"Oh," said Caroline. "But I thought I saw a man drive away from the house as I came along this morning, a fair man, thirtyish."

They had paused in the hall and Miss Masters continued to use a confidential tone as she said: "That must have been Mr. Lessing. I believe he comes and goes rather a lot. Travels in something or other — what they call a Rep. nowadays." Her kindly little eyes sharpened. "Are you feeling all right?" she asked.

Caroline stared at her blankly for a moment, then she faltered: "Excuse me. I don't think I'll have any coffee. I — I feel rather sick."

She turned and went stumbling upstairs, unconscious of the watching eyes of the concerned and interested Miss Masters.

"What's the matter, Mabel?" asked Miss Benson, sharply, joining her in the hall, and bent her head to listen to her friend's murmured reply.

'Mr. Lessing,' Caroline was thinking. 'Mr. Lessing, who comes and goes rather a lot.' Why had she never thought of that? Because the idea would have been too humiliating? Or because she was still something of a silly little innocent?

A picture of the generously proportioned, white skinned, blonde haired Mrs. Lessing formed in her mind. Did she represent Gordon's real taste in women? The very opposite of her slight, dark, rather almond eyed self! Or did he hanker after variety? One thing was clear. He liked his females to keep themselves and probably help support him, too.

After the disillusionment of the last few days, she was surprised at the sharpness of her distress. It was not lessened by the voice of her deeper self that told her it really served her right, or by the knowledge that it was hurt pride more than wounded love that was causing her pain.

What she had felt for Gordon had been love of a kind, but based mainly on physical attraction and a willing subjection to the charm he had deliberately exerted to win her. The spell had been wearing thin even before this nightmare had started. If she had been less lonely, more experienced, she would never have succumbed, she knew.

She had been a fool. But Gordon had been worse than a fool. Her thoughts flew again to the story Neil had told her. Could his dark suspicions have any foundation in truth, after all? Was her husband one of those men who prey on silly, fond, credulous women? Even to the point of murdering them if they tried to break away before they had been plucked?

She shivered as if with cold and

then started as a gentle tap sounded on the door.

"Who's there?" she asked anxiously.

"Mrs. Bannister?" said the voice of an unknown man. "Are you all right?"

Before she could answer, the door opened and the elderly, shrewd eyed Dr Hardwick entered and closed it softly behind him.

"I'm sorry if I intrude," he said, looking with a steady professional stare at Caroline. "But the two ladies downstairs were anxious about you and insisted that I should take a look at you. I am — or was — I've retired now — a medical man, and I haven't quite forgotten all the tricks of the trade. Is there anything I can do for you?"

"No, thank you," murmured Caroline, sitting up and straightening her skirt, for she had been sprawling on the bed in an abandonment of shame and anger and grief. She added, a little afraid of that penetrating gaze: "I've been under some stress lately, and I suddenly felt a little shakey. The heat perhaps — "

"Ah yes. It gets a little stuffy in the dining-room sometimes. I've told my niece about it before now," said the doctor, sitting down uninvited in the solitary armchair, but keeping his eyes on her.

"Your niece?" said Caroline, with a new interest in him.

He nodded. "Mrs. Lessing." He added: "But I live here as an ordinary paying guest. I prefer it. Solves all the house-keeping problems of a lone old man. At the same time I'm company for her." He smiled with a trace of irony. "And can give her a semblance of masculine support when her husband's away, Which he often is — on business."

To her dismay, Caroline felt a burning blush flooding her face and neck as she thought of that husband being her husband too, of his shuttling back and forth between the two of them, probably inventing the same explanations and excuses for each of them, making love to them in turn.

"I — I didn't know Mrs. Lessing was married. I thought at first she was a widow," she remarked, without thinking very clearly what she was saying, unable to meet Dr Hardwick's eyes.

"Only a grass one," he replied lightly.

"It's hard for a woman," she murmured, as she felt the blush receding. And then asked a question that had been knocking at the door of her mind from the beginning. "How long have they been married?"

He showed no surprise.

"It must be about ten years now," he said. "Time for her to have got used to all his departures and arrivals."

"Ten years?" repeated Caroline.

Ten years! So she had never been legally married to Gordon herself! Oddly enough, the thought brought a certain relief after the first shock.

"I've no desire to pry, my dear," said the old doctor quietly. "But I guess, by your reaction just now, that the cause of the stress you mentioned is matrimonial trouble of some sort."

"Yes," Caroline admitted.

For a moment she was tempted to pour the whole story out to him. But caution halted the impulse. She must face Gordon first, positively identify him as her own bigamously married husband. Neil, too, was concerned in this. For the marriage to Rosalind Fuller must have been as illegal as her own, and Gordon's inheritance of her money an appalling confidence trick, even if he had not contrived her drowning.

"Well," said Dr. Hardwick, rising, "I lay no claim to being a psychiatrist — the profession does as much harm as good in my opinion. I'm all for surgery myself."

Suddenly there was something formidable about him, a hardness and toughness under the smooth white hair and quiet manner, as he nodded at her.

"Yes, there's a lot to be said for the

knife," he told her. "A clean decisive cut. There'll be bleeding, of course, but it'll soon stop."

He gave Caroline another little nod — of encouragement this time, then paused in the doorway to add: "I should take a couple of aspirins before you go to bed. They're a mild sedative. And good luck, my dear."

The door closed softly behind him.

He was right, of course, Caroline decided. The knife was best. A complete severance. Divorce. But could there be divorce where there had been no true marriage? She thought not. So she was free already. Free! It was a strange feeling. Not entirely pleasant or unpleasant. Rather a naked feeling. Something to get used to.

What was she to do in the meanwhile? Could she stay here, even for the night, in a house where Gordon was presumably master? And he might return at any time. She had no proof that he had gone back to Willow Lodge.

Suddenly the idea of meeting Gordon here, and surprising him in his treachery, when she was alone and unsupported and he was in the midst of his real family, frightened her. Suppose his wife knew all the time what he was doing, and didn't mind so long as she profited by it. Suppose she merely despised his victims. Suppose Gordon really was a murderer.

She could go to the police. Bigamy was a crime. But first she must identify the criminal. So far all she could say was that she had seen her husband leave this house and one of the guests had told her it must have been Mr. Lessing she had seen.

Suppose it was a mistake.

She went on sitting on the side of the bed as it dawned on her that this was a distinct possibility. She had been going on hearsay, after all. Hearsay and circumstantial evidence of a not too convincing kind. But it had convinced her. Until this moment she had had no doubts of Gordon's guilt. Now she did not acquit him, only thought of the Scottish verdict of 'not proven'.

If only there was somebody she could confide in! Somebody who would give her advice and support!

There was Neil Fuller, of course. He was probably still in Fulhaven, and already knew something of the problems that were troubling her. And, as she had thought before, if Gordon had bigamously married Rosalind was rightfully concerned.

Her distrust of Neil was modified now by her need. At the thought of pouring out her story to him, her heart lifted a little.

But could she find him? She could try.

She hurried to the wardrobe, took out her coat and put it on, then, pausing only to snatch up her handbag, went from the room and quietly — almost furtively — down the stairs and out of the house.

10

THE wind had died down with sunset, but it was working up again. The chains of lights that decorated the darkness on the Promenade were swaying a little and the bushes in the shrubbery at the end of Down Way were rustling and whispering. A few prematurely withered leaves from the taller trees skipped along the pavement, and a piece of paper, blown out of one of the litter-baskets, drifted over the grass like a tiny ghost. Over the invisible sea black clouds hid the stars, but a few shone here and there on the water, marking buoys and anchored ships.

There were only a few people about, for it was not an evening for sitting out of doors, or for strolling by the sea. Most of the residents and visitors were lingering over coffee in their hotels and guesthouses and homes, or cosily watching television.

One or two hardy folk, however, walked briskly along the Promenade, with coat collars turned up, while accompanying dogs bounded ahead or lingered behind to enjoy a sniff.

Neil had not said definitely that he was staying in Fulhaven, thought Caroline. Only that it depended. On what, she wondered? On whether or not he could track down Gordon? If he was still here where would he be staying?

She passed the Grand Hotel and the Majestic, a faint scent of roses wafting to her nostrils from the beds in front of them. Somehow she didn't think that Neil would be patronizing either of those rather opulent looking establishments. But outside the Ocean Hotel she hesitated and finally turned. Pushing through the swing-doors, she crossed the deeply carpeted hall to the desk.

No, said the clerk, her friend Mr.

Neil Fuller was not one of their guests.

She received the same reply from the Promenade Hotel and the Seaview Hotel as well as the Channel Hotel and the Hotel France.

Her courage began to fail her at the thought of all the hotels and guesthouses that remained, in any of which Neil might be. There was the Fulhaven itself, she remembered, down by the harbour. She ought to enquire there. Perhaps he preferred being near boats to this strictly-for-the-tourists area.

But she continued to walk along the Promenade, inspired by a vague hope that she might meet Neil by chance as she had done that afternoon, this time braving the wind under the festooned lights.

The night seemed full of elemental sound. As each gust died down she could hear the mumble and muted roar of the sea down below, then the trees would heave great sighs, and a moaning and whining would set up from unseen stanchions and wires.

The dog exercisers and fresh-air enthusiasts who passed Caroline looked curiously at the small woman who walked with her coat collar up and her hands in her pockets, a scarf whipping about her pale face, as if wondering why she had no escort in this holiday town and not even the excuse of a dog to bring her out. But once it was she who stared. It was when a man in a beret and a belted raincoat came striding towards her and she recognized him as Dr. Hardwick as he drew near. He passed her without a glance, however, his eyes gazing straight ahead and his half bitter half humorous mouth set.

She gave him the beginnings of a greeting, cut short when she saw his unnoticing expression, and looked round after him, till he turned into the entrance of the Marine Private Hotel, which had a Bar that was open to non-residents, she remembered.

She walked on, though without much

purpose now. The chains of lights had come to an end and there was only an occasional lamp standard to light the windy darkness. There were no more hotels, either, only a high wall, bounding either a park or some private grounds, she judged. She met no pedestrians now, but came upon one or two parked cars, still by the kerbside, with or without occupants it was hard to tell.

She was beginning to feel tired, and when she came to a glassed-in shelter facing the invisible sea she paused, with the idea of resting in it for a few minutes. But perhaps, she thought, it was already occupied by a pair of lovers, wanting seclusion.

She branched off to the narrow path that passed in front of it near the edge of the cliff, that was a mere shallow incline here, for her way had led her steadily downhill. The roar of the waves was much louder from this new position, but a small headland cut her off from the force of the wind. It would certainly not be unpleasant to sit a while in the shelter. But first she must make sure she was not intruding on the lovers she had imagined in there.

The nearest standard was some distance off and the light that reached her from it thin and weak, but it was enough to show her that the shape she saw huddled in a corner of the seat had not sufficient bulk to make two persons, however closely embracing.

She strained her eyes to see better. And now she could make out a pair of legs stretched out and a head hanging forward. Was the man asleep? It *was* a man, she decided, though sometimes it was hard to tell. A tramp perhaps, taking advantage of a roof and three walls at least, for his night's lodging. Maybe it would not be wise to go in and share his solitude. It was really rather a lonely spot, and if one cried out the chances were nobody would hear, what with the noises of the sea and the wind and the distance from the main part of the Promenade.

She had gone discreetly past when the thought struck her that it could be Neil sitting there in the darkness alone. It was improbable, of course, but it was certainly possible. How ironic, if she was running away from the very man she was looking for!

She remembered then the pocket-torch in her handbag. If she went back and switched it on under pretence of illuminating the path in front of the shelter, it might throw enough light to enable her to make certain that it wasn't Neil, at least.

She got the torch out, switched it on and went back, improving on her first idea by pretending to look for some object on the ground in front of her, as she walked. The ray of light shone ahead, revealing intimate details of the path small stones and cracks and edgings of grass and tiny plants. Now it lit up the legs of the man in the shelter, and a paper-bag and sweet-wrapping the wind must have blown against his feet. On one brown toe-cap a deep pink rose petal was lying. He must have been keeping very still for that to have stayed there, she thought, and manipulated the torch so that its ray went higher.

It crept up the fawn coloured trousers, and open jacket, over the smart, cream-coloured sweater till it reached the breast and hanging head. Then she gave a thin, quavering cry and her nerveless fingers dropped the little torch. It rolled away, still shining but now illuminating only the ground again. But the sight she had seen before it fell was imprinted on her mind for ever.

The man in the shelter was Gordon. Gordon, with his hands hanging limply at his sides, his chin resting on his chest, and just below it a dark hole in the centre of what looked like a great red flower. His eyes, opened in a fixed stare, seemed to be gazing at the freakish rose petal on his toe-cap.

But he was not seeing anything. He would never see anything again. Caroline had looked at the face of death three times in her life, and she knew that this was a fourth occasion. And this time it was the face of violent death.

Trembling, she stooped and picked up the torch, then forced herself to turn it upon the still figure in the shelter again, for incredulity had followed the first horrible shock of conviction. Perhaps an overwrought imagination had deceived her. Perhaps there was some eccentric pattern on the pullover. Perhaps it wasn't even Gordon.

But such desperate straw-clutching was abandoned as the ray mercilessly picked out the bullet-wound, the blood, the drooping head, the pallid face and fixed sightless stare.

Somewhere ahead in the darkness a girl's laugh sounded above the low roar of the sea and all the little noises of the wind.

Caroline switched off the torch abruptly, turned and hurried away, stumbling along the now dimly lighted path. She did not think of calling for help. Gordon was beyond it, as far as this world was concerned. She wanted only to put as much distance as possible between herself and the dead man, for she did not doubt that murder had been done.

More and more she had come to realize that she knew nothing of the man she had married, that his true personality had been hidden from her. But she could not think that he had committed suicide. Besides, if he had shot himself the weapon would have been either still in his hand or on the ground close by. And it was not.

She shivered, feeling throughly cold now, partly with shock. She pitied Gordon, as she would have pitied a stranger, or an animal, that had died in such a way, but she felt no grief. It was as if her past association with him had been a dream — a dream that had ended in nightmare. If she could get home, back to Willow Lodge, where life had been real for her before she had met Gordon, then perhaps she would begin to feel awake again, she thought.

Mixed with this instinctive desire for the security of the nest, the cave, was a very rational fear of being involved in a horrible crime, perhaps even suspected of having had a part in it. Imagination and logic told her that she had had both motive and opportunity, and the police might well think that her behaviour over the last few days had been a likely prelude to murder. She felt a great thankfulness that she had registered at Regency House as Mrs. Bannister.

The wind tugged at her skirt and whipped her scarf-end about her face, and it began to rain a little as she hurried along the Promenade, past the hotels with their shining windows and glimpses of carefree holiday makers, under the cheerful festoons of light. All the time she expected to hear an outcry behind her, sounds indicating that the dead man had been found, calls for her to stop, perhaps even the siren of a police-car.

She gave a little sob of relief when she reached her car, parked at the kerb side, under a chain of gently swaying lights. Now she had only to get in it and drive through the darkness till she reached home. But she checked herself as she was about to feel in her handbag for her keys. No. That would never do. If she didn't return to Regency House there would be enquiries after her, a hue and cry, perhaps an actual linking of her disappearance with the mysterious death of the man in the shelter, the man who had been driving away from the guesthouse that morning as she had arrived, and who was, she was fairly certain, the husband of the proprietress.

So she must go back and produce a perfectly plausible reason for packing her things and leaving at once. Illness? She had drawn notice by her sickly appearance and had claimed to be under stress when talking to Dr. Hardwick. But that wouldn't do. She could hardly set off to drive to London, where she was supposed to live, if she was really ill.

She must try to control her chaotic thoughts and invent some fool-proof story. She should be able to do it. Wasn't it her profession? Only in real life she had always been a very truthful person. Could she act convincingly? The thing to do, of course, was make use of her state of shock without revealing the true cause of her horror and dismay. An accident then. Not to herself but to somebody dear to her. A child? Yes, that was it. She must say that she had telephoned to her home from a public callbox, just to make sure all was well there without her, and learned that her little son, Jeremy, had fallen and broken an arm and was crying for her. She must, of course, go to him at once. Her sister was staying at the house to care for him, but at such a time a child needed his mother. She was sure Mrs. Lessing would understand.

Mrs. Lessing appeared to do so,

though her placidity was not disturbed. Caroline had summoned her from a dimly lit lounge, where she was sitting among her guests looking at television. Only the doctor and the two oldish young men were absent.

As Caroline made her fictional excuses, with a volubility not at all natural to her, saying that she had hoped to spend a few days here in peace and quiet in order to think something out, but of course Jeremy came first, and of course she would pay for her room, she wondered what change would show in those calm blue eyes if she were to tell what she had seen in the shelter such a short time ago. Did that full seductive bosom ever become agitated? That voluptuous mouth tighten in anger or suffering?

This woman could be called her rival, but she felt no jealousy of her. Only a vague pity and curiosity.

She escaped upstairs to pack, resisting a mad momentary desire to blurt out that the husband they shared was dead — murdered. She threw her belongings into her case and hurried downstairs again, where Mrs. Lessing was waiting to shake hands and speed her parting guest.

"Such a pity!" she murmured. "The forecast is fine for tomorrow. I hope you'll come again when your little boy is better."

She stood politely at the open door till Caroline had reached the gate, then, with a wave of one large white hand, stepped back and shut the door. Caroline could imagine her returning with feline satisfaction to the cosy lounge and the bright images, as she carried her case through the wind and the rain to the car, parked now as near to the house as other vehicles at the kerbside would allow.

There was a moment of panic when the engine refused to start. Occasionally it did this, she didn't know why. She had intended to take it to a garage as soon as Gordon got back with his car. How appalling if her procrastination was punished now by the engine's complete breakdown! What should she do? She broke out in a sweat at the idea. But her desperate twiddles abruptly paid off and there was a comforting and familiar purr. The windscreen wipers swept to and fro and her blurred vision of the lights of Fulhaven sharpened and cleared.

She thought about Gordon's car again, as she drove down to the harbour. Was it parked anywhere near the shelter, where she had seen the two or three stationary cars earlier? She had not noticed, for it was Neil she was looking for then. But could Gordon be traced to Willow Lodge and herself through his ownership of the vehicle? He had told her it belonged to his firm and was registered as theirs. But Dobson and Perks certainly didn't own it. She knew that now.

Once away from the town and out in the open country there was not a lot of traffic on the road. Caroline drove like an automaton, while the greater part of her mind was occupied in going over and over again her shattering experience. And now she went beyond the fact of Gordon's violent death and considered how it could have happened. Had Neil Fuller come up with his ex-brother-in-law there in the shelter and accused him of being a wife-murderer? And had Gordon's response provoked him to such an extent that he had killed him then and there? It was said that red hair went with a passionate temper, but she had always thought this as untrue as most generalizations. And it seemed that Gordon had been shot, which meant that who ever killed him had carried a gun already loaded and prepared for use. And surely that meant premeditation.

But she had suspected Neil of searching for Gordon, had believed — or half believed that he had tracked her here to Fulhaven on the chance that she would lead him to her husband. So why should she reject the idea that he carried a weapon?

Because she couldn't think of Neil as a killer. Easier to imagine him simply hitting out with his fists and prepared to take his enemy's blows in return. But she had been fooled already by one man. Why should she think she was any judge of another? And she knew nothing about Neil Fuller — except what he had chosen to tell her. He *must* have been the murderer. It stood to reason.

The windscreen-wipers swept to and fro, the car ate up the miles, her lights shone on the glistening ribbon of the wet road, bringing momentarily to view wet grass, dripping trees, brick walls a richer red for their wetness, gleaming windows, soaking hedges, villages settling to sleep.

It had stopped raining by the time she reached Oxridge. As she let herself into Willow Lodge and switched on the lights, Colonel came to meet her from the kitchen, yawning and stretching luxuriously and blinking narrowed eyes. It was wonderful to be home at first,

221

but soon the quiet house seemed full of whispers and shadows, ghosts of Gordon and ghosts of her past and happier self. She poured herself a tot of brandy and carried it upstairs to one of the spare bedrooms reserved for a guest who never had come, for she shuddered away from the thought of spending the night in the room she had shared with Gordon and seeing his empty bed beside her.

She drank the brandy while she made up her new bed, remembering that she had spent the night in this room once or twice when she had come to visit her godmother in her girlhood. Then she flung off her clothes and lay down, switching off the light and covering her face with the bedclothes, like a child afraid of what she might see.

But this could not shut out the mental vision of the dead man, with his ghastly pallor, bloodstained chest and blank eyes staring at the rose petal on his shoe. It was early morning when she fell asleep at last.

Surprisingly, she slept heavily and dreamlessly till past eight o'clock. But memory returned with consciousness, disturbingly enough but not with the horrifying images of the night before. Daylight lessened the effect of her experience, daylight and some hours of healthy slumber. But it was still in the forefront of her mind and she pulled on her housecoat and hurried downstairs to see if the newspaper had come. It had, and she took it into the kitchen, anxiously scanning the pages as she walked, nearly falling over Colonel, who wanted to rub around her legs. Then, ignoring his demands to be let out, she spread the paper on the table and went over it carefully, column by column, page by page.

At last she was convinced that there was no mention in it of a dead man found in a shelter at Fulhaven. Could it be that he was still sitting there, with birds hopping about his feet, and flies settling on him, and sunshine slanting in to spotlight the horror of him? Or was it that he had been discovered too late for this edition?

She glanced at the clock and saw that it was still only twenty past eight. She would have to wait till nine o'clock for the radio news. She put on the electric kettle and made herself some tea, let the cat in again and fed him, toasted some bread and buttered it, feeling that she couldn't eat with any appetite but must take something.

As she sat at the table, sipping and brooding, her scalp pricked and a shiver ran down her spine as she heard the sound of the front door opening and closing. Who but herself and Gordon had a key? Only Mrs. Hedges, who never came in on a Saturday.

Had she made some terrible mistake? Was the man in the shelter some stranger after all, with a superficial resemblance to Gordon in death? The thought flashed through her mind, to be banished instantly as she recognized her

Help's heavy footsteps in the passage outside.

The next moment Mrs. Hedges' round face and stout form appeared in the doorway, her pale eyes wide with surprise.

"Why, you're back then, Mrs. Lane!" she exclaimed. "I come to feed His Nibs, like you asked me." There was a hint of reproach in her tone.

"I'd forgotten what we arranged," gasped Caroline.

"I give you a bit of a shock, didn't I?" said the Daily, looking at her curiously. "Well, I didn't expect to see you, neither. Thought you was going away for a few days."

"Yes," said Caroline, recovering. "Yes, I was. But I changed my mind, because of the weather, and — and not feeling well. I came back last night."

"Oh, I'm sorry you're poorly, Mrs. Lane," said Mrs. Hedges, forgiving her employer and looking at her with the usual speculation. "I'd look after meself if I was you. Well, seeing as I'm not needed I'll be getting back. There's three and fourpence to pay on this little lot, please. Bought it last night, but it's been in me fridge, so it should be all right. Half a pound of heart and a nice piece of coley. That should see puss over the weekend. And there are them tins of Cat Joy in the larder."

Caroline thanked her, without quite taking in what she had said, for already it was nine o'clock. She was afraid to switch on the radio, however, in case Mrs. Hedges decided to stop and listen to the news. It would be too great a strain on her acting abilities, she thought, if she heard a report of Gordon's murder and dared not show her feelings. And the woman was sure to comment and dwell on the subject. It was just the kind of thing that would enthrall her.

When the door had closed on her broad back, after more brief civilities, Caroline hurried to switch on. She was just in time. There was the tail end of a piece of political news and then:

"A man was found shot in a shelter in Fulhaven, in the early hours of the morning. He has been identified as a local resident, Graham Lessing. The police are treating the case as one of murder."

That was all. But it was enough for Caroline. She turned the set off and sat staring into space, knowing that all her suspicions were now confirmed. Gordon had been a liar and a bigamist — perhaps worse — and he was dead. It might be that she, herself, had had a lucky escape. She thought of Rosalind Fuller's drowning off the coast of Brittainy, with no witness except the man who was not legally her husband. Did she perhaps suspect the truth? If so, that would have been a reason for seeing that her mouth was closed for ever, in addition to the motive of greed.

She thought of the cutting she had found in Gordon's desk, advertizing the lonely cottage by the dangerous sea, and shuddered.

Well, she would never know for certain now what Gordon's intentions towards her had been. But, with her new knowledge, it was a relief to think she would never see him again. She must wipe him out of her life as if he had never been. She would have to think up a story of a quarrel and separation to give her acquaintances and few friends. Only to Mary Green, perhaps, when she returned from her holiday, she would tell the whole truth. She could trust Mary. She need not say much to the others. Her reticence would be put down to hurt feelings and her usual shyness.

She bathed and dressed and did a few domestic chores. It was fresh and sweet outside, after the rain, and she went into the garden and cut off a few dead flowers near the front gate. A neighbour passed and invited her in for coffee, but Caroline excused herself by saying she had a great deal to do."

"Husband not back yet?" asked the

woman, a mother who was beginning to feel that she was no longer necessary to her grown up children and hungry to be wanted.

"No," said Caroline, and had no need to act a change of tone and facial expression.

She saw the woman's eyes sharpen with curiosity, and knew that the seed she had wanted to sow had fallen on fertile ground already.

As the day went by a strange feeling of peace gradually descended on her. There was no need to wonder any more when Gordon would be coming home or what he was doing. No need to worry about his likes and dislikes. No being torn this way and that by doubts and loyalties. It seemed as if there was a slow expansion of her personality, as if her true self had shrunk and put up barriers and now could stretch out to know a new freedom.

She opened some tins of food for her lunch, ate it from a tray in the garden, then went into her writing-room and began to work on her book. It struck her afterwards that her behaviour was extraordinary, in the circumstances. How could she have concentrated so well and written so easily? How could she have successfully shut out for that time, the image that had haunted her mind earlier? How could she have been so out of touch with reality as to have imagined the nightmare was over and done with? But the mind has its own way of protecting itself and healing its hurts.

A ring at the front door brought her back to consciousness of her surroundings with a jerk. She looked at her watch. It was ten to five and she was aware of feeling thirsty and nervously exhausted. She must put the kettle on as soon as the caller had gone, and make herself some tea. Or perhaps ask whoever was ringing to come in and share it with her.

She opened the door with no misgivings at all, and felt as if a dark pit had suddenly opened at her feet and she was in danger of dropping into it. On the step, upright and alert, stood a young, peak-capped policeman. She could see his official car outside the gate.

"Mrs. Lane?" he asked, with a polite little smile that showed excellent teeth.

She nodded wordlessly.

"I wonder if I might have a word with you, please."

She nodded again, and opened the door wider.

He came inside, removing his cap and wiping his shoes on the mat. She walked like an automaton ahead of him, back to her writing-room and sat down, motioning him to another chair. It had seemed natural to go back to the room she had come out of.

He sat down, looking about him in an interested way, at the desk and the typewriter and the pages of typescript. His observant glance took in the shelf of bright jacketed books with the name Carole Bannister on their spines. Then his eyes focussed on her again.

Caroline had had time to pull herself together. She knew that her manner must have seemed very odd — if not downright guilty. She ought to have asked him what he wanted, why he had called.

"What is it?" she asked abruptly.

"The Fulhaven police have asked us to make some enquiries for them, madame," he answered, with a frank and open expression on his smooth young face. "They asked us to call and see you, as you were in Fulhaven yesterday."

11

"**H**OW did you know?" asked Caroline, staring at him as if he were some incongruously garbed magician.

He smiled again, looking rather pleased, as if he had brought off a successful trick.

"They traced your car," he said. "One of their men noticed it along by the Promenade and took a note of the number in order to keep a check on it, on account of some parking rule."

Caroline remembered Mrs. Lessing telling her that the Fiat could be parked where she had left it so long as she took it away once in twenty-four hours.

"I see," she said bleakly.

The young policeman stopped smiling. He was thinking that this Mrs. Lane was an abrupt and unfriendly person, with a face of curious inscrutability.

But perhaps it was because she was a writer and he had interrupted her in the mysterious throes of composition.

"I don't know whether you're aware of it, madame, but there was a man murdered in a shelter at the end of the Promenade last night," he said, unbuttoning his jacket pocket and taking out a notebook and pen.

"Yes. I heard about it on the news," said Caroline, and then, with an attempt at showing some natural interest: "At — at the end of the Promenade, was it?"

"That's right," nodded the policeman. "And we're wondering if you heard or saw anything unusual yesterday evening, while you were in Fulhaven. What time did you drive away from the Promenade?"

"I left — it must have been before nine o'clock," she answered. "And I don't think I heard or saw anything unusual."

"I noticed, madame, that you say 'I' and not 'we'," remarked the young man. "Your husband wasn't with you, I take it."

For a terrible moment Caroline wondered if this could be a trap of some sort. But the young man looked guileless enough.

"My husband is away," she said.

"I see. Did you walk along the Promenade at all yesterday evening?" he said, making a brief note.

She shook her head. "It was a windy night. Not the sort of weather for walking, and when one is by oneself — I — I walked to the car from — from where I had dinner, of course," she said.

"And where was that, madame?" asked the young man, with pen poised.

Caroline named the hotel where she had had lunch. "It's along the front," she explained.

He nodded as he wrote, then looked up, bright-eyed. "And you can't remember hearing anything like a car backfiring, for instance?" he said.

She tried not to show that the

question upset her, shaking her head again quickly. "I don't remember noticing anything like that," she said. "Of course, the wind was making rather a noise, and if I was indoors at the time — "

He gave her a quick look and she nerved herself to ask him a question.

"What time was it?" she blurted.

"Was what?" he said smoothly.

"The sound that might have been taken for a car backfiring," she said, holding his gaze.

"They're still making enquiries," he said.

Somebody could have heard the fatal shot without realizing what it was, she thought. That was what he meant. But did they really not know the exact time of Gordon's death?

"Were you alone all the time in Fulhaven, Mrs. Lane? Or did you visit friends, or meet anybody you knew, there?" he asked.

Caroline thought of Neil Fuller and hesitated for an imperceptible moment before answering: "I was alone all the time. It was a lovely day and I went down there because I fancied a breath of sea air and wanted solitude to think out something that was bothering me."

He glanced with respect at the typewriter and nodded understandingly, closed the notebook and stood up.

Just as she thought her ordeal was over he flung a final question at her. "Do you know anybody called Lessing, Mrs. Lane?"

She sat for a moment, willing herself to be calm and controlled. Then she shook her head thoughtfully. "No," she said slowly. "No, I don't." And she rose, though her legs felt weak under her.

"Thank you very much. You've been most helpful, madame," said the young man politely, replacing the notebook and pen. "I won't take up any more of your time."

He cast another lingering, respectful glance at the desk and the shelf of books, then walked to the door.

When he had gone, Caroline leaned for a moment against the table in the hall, feeling faint with relief. She was shaken out of her mood of euphoria. She realized now that she could not cut herself off from what had happened. And how frighteningly thorough the police had been. To trace her, thinking she was a mere uninvolved tripper, on the bare chance that she might have heard or seen something they could connect with the crime!

She was glad she had not mentioned her meeting with Neil. If she had done so it might have led to the police investigating him a little too closely.

If he had killed Gordon it was a terrible thing he had done, but she did not want to be the one to point the finger. Let the truth come out, if it must, but by some other means. Neil might actually have thought that he was firing the bullet on her behalf as well as to revenge his dead sister, though God knew she had not wanted murder done.

She was making the tea when a startling possibility occurred to her. Suppose the police traced Neil as they had traced her, by means of his car, and suppose he told them he had met her in Fulhaven yesterday. It would contradict her own statement that she was alone all the time. She could say that the chance encounter had slipped her memory, but would the police believe her? Mightn't they start questioning the rest of her statement? Or they might imagine she and Neil were having an illicit affair, and then, if ever Graham Lessing should be identified as Gordon Lane also —

She put down the teapot she was holding and began to search for the piece of paper on which Neil had written his phone number. She found it finally in the pocket of her car-coat, and went to the telephone in her writing-room, staring at the figures and at the '01' that preceded them. It was a London number, then.

Would Neil be available? The chances

were he was staying the weekend in Fulhaven — if he was innocent. But if he wasn't, wouldn't he want to put as much distance as possible between himself and the scene of the crime?

The thought chilled her and she hesitated, reluctant to put her idea to the test. But she had decided not to condemn him in any case, hadn't she?

She picked up the telephone and dialed a little clumsily. The ringing tone sounded for a short period, and then:

"Mrs. Fuller speaking," said a clear feminine voice, with a slight North Country accent.

Mrs. Fuller! Somehow, Caroline had not imagined Neil with a wife. For a moment she was tempted to replace the receiver, but she resisted the urge.

"Is Mr. Neil Fuller there please?" she said.

"I'm afraid my son is out at the moment," answered the voice. "Who — Oh, I think I hear him coming in now. Who is speaking, please?"

"Will you tell him it's Caroline," said Caroline cautiously.

"Caroline!" said Mrs. Fuller. She sounded pleased for some reason. "What a pretty name! And one doesn't hear it often. Hold on, please, and I'll tell Neil you want to speak to him."

'She thinks I'm a new girl friend of her son's,' thought Caroline, as she waited. 'She sounds rather a dear. Poor thing! If she knew what I suspect!' For the fact that Neil was not in Fulhaven still counted against him, according to the little test she had invented.

"Hallo Caroline," said his voice in her ear, sounding so calm and normal that she began to doubt some of her conclusions at once. "What can I do for you?"

"I can't talk over the phone. Could we meet somewhere, as soon as possible, please?" she said urgently.

He gave a curious little laugh. "I take it something has happened. Because I got the impression you weren't at all pleased with our meeting yesterday,"

241

he said in a low voice.

Something happened! She had to make her mind accept the possibility that he hadn't an inkling of Gordon's death. And if he was merely pretending then she must pretend with him.

"Yes," she said. "Something has happened. Something dreadful, Neil." (Was it really the first time she had called him that?)

"I see." His tone had changed. "Look. Can you have dinner with me this evening?" he asked. "You can? Good. Do you know the Merry Pilgrim? It's on the road between your place and Brendhurst Common. Could you meet me there in the cocktail lounge in a couple of hours time? We can have drinks before we eat and you can tell me all about it."

"Yes," said Caroline. "Thank you. And Neil, will you be leaving soon?"

Would there be time for the police to call on him before he set out?

"Almost at once," he answered. "See you soon then."

Caroline knew the Merry Pilgrim by sight, though she had never been inside before. Gordon had not been given to taking her out to such places, and she realized why now. The number of cars outside and in the car-park rather alarmed her. It did not promise an opportunity for quiet talk within.

The road house was a timbered building of genuine antiquity, that had been renovated and 'improved' by the syndicate that owned it, within the limitations of the laws for the protection of ancient monuments. When Caroline pushed open the door of the cocktail lounge and entered she was appalled by the roar of conversation that greeted her. Then she saw Neil's red head above the throng, as he rose from a small table by the wall.

"I'm afraid this wasn't a very good idea of mine after all," he said with a smile, when she had reached him. "I'd forgotten what the place is like on a Saturday night. All the tables in the restaurant are booked, too."

"Never mind," she consoled him, raising her voice to be heard above the babble. "I'm not hungry."

"Aren't you?" he said, looking at her quizzically. "I am rather. Besides, one can't invite a lady out to dinner and then tell her there's nothing doing. I'll find somewhere else. In the meanwhile, what will you have to drink?"

Caroline asked for sherry and he made his way to the bar, saying that they would be there all night if they depended on the two overworked waiters. She was glad he was tall, she thought, watching him, then wondered at herself. What did his tallness matter to her? For a moment she had felt like any ordinary woman out with an attractive man.

They shouted a few unimportant remarks at each other while they sipped their drinks. It was impossible to hold any serious conversation under the circumstances. Caroline refused a second glass of sherry.

"Let's go, shall we?" she said, and

he nodded and helped her on with her coat.

Outside, the air felt extraordinarily fresh and sweet, and the descending twilight full of peace. Caroline rebelled at the thought of another noisy, crowded hostelry.

"Neil," she said impulsively, "if you're really hungry, perhaps you'd like to come home with me. I can only offer you an omelette, but we can talk in peace and quiet."

He looked at her oddly, as if weighing up her true motive. Then he nodded.

"Thank you," he said, smiling. "I'm partial to omelettes, as a matter of fact. You must let me chop the chives, or what ever you put in them. Lead the way and I'll follow."

As she unlocked her front door, a little while later, and held it open for him to enter, the thought came to her that she might be doing a dangerous thing in letting into her house a man of whom she knew so little, but whom she suspected of being a murderer. Suppose he decided that he would get rid of her, too, because she had seen him at Fulhaven yesterday. Who would hear her if she screamed for help in this quiet place?

She gave a cry as something whipped silently past her legs. But it was only Colonel, hurrying indoors while he had the chance.

Neil smiled at the cat, who turned in the hall to stare at him as he entered.

"Nice puss!" he murmured, snapping his fingers. "Come here."

Disdaining to respond to an enticement he evidently thought only suited to a dog, Colonel stalked away to the kitchen to finish the snack he had thoughtfully left in his dish for such a moment.

It was Neil who suggested that they had their meal in the kitchen. She found that he meant his offer to help with the cooking, for he chopped parsley and beat the eggs for her efficiently, while she washed lettuce and sliced up cucumber and tomato.

"What was it you wanted to say to me?" he asked abruptly, glancing across at her, as she placed a bowl of apples and some crispbread on the table.

"I'll tell you when we've eaten," answered Caroline, avoiding his eyes.

She wished she need never speak of the terrible thing that had happened, that she could wipe it completely from her memory, and Gordon himself with it.

"That was good," said Neil some twenty minutes later, laying down his knife and fork and taking up an apple. He began to pare it with a fruit knife. "And this is all very cosy. I suppose your husband isn't likely to walk in on us now and suspect the worst? Don't think I'll mind if he does. In fact, I should rather welcome it."

Caroline stared at him. Was he speaking sincerely or only pretending? She found she wanted passionately the former to be true.

"Gordon's dead," she blurted.

His fingers were suddenly still and he

gave her a look of startled enquiry.

"What?" he said. "Since when?"

"Since last night," she told him.

He frowned. "Are you sure?"

She nodded wordlessly.

"Well, I can't pretend to be sorry. But I can see it's been a shock to you. What was it, an accident? Where did it happen? I suppose the police notified you," said Neil, firing off questions and comments without waiting for any response from her.

"He was shot — in a shelter in Fulhaven," she said, when he paused at last. And she wondered if it was really news to him.

"Shot? In a shelter? But that was on the news. And the name wasn't Lane — or Longton," said Neil, looking at her strangely. "It was — what was it?"

"Lessing," said Caroline. "Graham Lessing. That's what he called himself in Fulhaven. He was married to a woman who ran a guesthouse. The wedding was ten years ago."

Neil's frown deepened. "But that's — Then Rosalind — " he stammered.

"Your sister couldn't have been legally his wife. Neither could I," Caroline told him. "I found it all out yesterday."

"Good God!" he exclaimed. "The bloody little twister! He invited murder. What happened exactly?"

She hesitated, feeling herself shrinking inwardly, as the scene in the shelter became vividly alive again to her.

"I went to the end of the Promenade," she said, squeezing her hands together. "I wanted to find you."

"To find me?" he said, surprised. "Why?"

"To tell you. To ask you what I should do," said Caroline. "And — and I shone my torch into the shelter and he was sitting there." She shuddered and covered her face with her hands. "Oh, it was horrible!" she muttered.

"I see," he said quietly, his expression stiff with what looked like shock.

"Where did you get the gun? Did you leave it behind?"

She sat up, her eyes widened and her jaw dropped slightly. "What do you mean?" Her voice came out high pitched and unlike itself. "*I* didn't kill him. He was dead when I found him. There was blood all over him." She shuddered again.

"Did you go to the police?" he asked, his eyes probing hers as if searching for the truth.

She shook her head. "No. I suppose I panicked," she admitted. "I was afraid of being suspected. And how right I was, judging by your reaction just now," she added bitterly. "I went back to the guesthouse and said my little boy had broken his arm and I had to go home at once. Then I drove back here."

"I didn't know you had a child," remarked Neil, staring.

"I haven't — thank God!" said Caroline.

"And you have no idea who killed

the fellow?" he asked, with doubt in his eyes.

Caroline hesitated again. Then, meeting his gaze steadily, she told him: "I rather thought *you* had, as a matter of fact."

She saw that thrust go home in the way he blinked and gave a little backward jerk of the head, but he said, again quite quietly: "I see. You evidently think I keep my anger hot a long time. Until the other day, I hadn't seen the man for five years, and I've never handled any sort of gun in all my life — except a toy one when I was about ten."

"Well, I've never even handled a toy one," said Caroline. "And I knew you were after him, and you obviously hated him still. It seemed to me that seeing him again must have revived all you had felt at the time of your sister's death."

He bit his lip then nodded reluctantly. "Yes," he admitted. "That's true in a way. It was seeing him so untouched by the past, and finding him married again to a girl who, in many particulars reminded me of Rosalind."

"Was she as simple and gullible as me?" asked Caroline bitterly.

He shook his head with a very slight smile. "She was rather unworldly, loyal and slow to think evil," he said. "And, of course, she had money of her own."

Caroline winced. Then she asked flatly: "Why did you have me followed to Fulhaven?"

"What?" he said sharply. "Of course I did no such thing. What gave you such an idea?"

"Well, why were you there?" said Caroline. "And *somebody* was having me followed. There was a man on a motor-bike who kept popping up. The same man who was at the Hand in Hand, fiddling with his lamp. Do you remember?" And she went on to recount all the circumstances of her drive down to the coast.

"That's odd," he remarked slowly.

"Are you sure the whole thing wasn't coincidence?"

"Do you know, I can't believe in quite so many coincidences," said Caroline. "He and you and I all happening to go to Fulhaven independently, and Gordon, too, happening to be there."

Neil frowned. "But didn't you go because you knew he was there?" he said. "That's certainly what *I* thought when I met you there."

"I didn't *know* it," said Caroline. "I found a Fulhaven address among his things. But let that pass. *You*, I suppose you're going to say, went there simply for your health."

For the first time he looked a little angry. "I went to Fulhaven because that was where I picked up his trail again, about five weeks ago. At least, it was on the Fulhaven train. I followed him out of the station here and heard him tell the taxi-driver this address. I would have investigated earlier, only I went to Spain for three weeks soon afterwards."

"Oh," said Caroline. She considered. "Yes. Gordon did go away by train about five weeks ago. His car was laid up and he wouldn't borrow mine. He went to Birmingham, he said."

"By way of Beachy Head, no doubt," said Neil dryly. "But what *he* was doing in Fulhaven we know now. That leaves the man with the motor-bike. I suppose he couldn't have been a policeman?"

"Why should the police have been interested in me?" asked Caroline. "If they'd followed me back home from Fulhaven there might have been some point in it. But they didn't need to do that. They'd got the number of my car and they traced me here by that."

"Traced you here?" said Neil, looking startled. "You don't mean the police have been here already!"

She nodded. "One very nice young constable, to ask if I'd noticed anything suspicious yesterday evening along the Promenade in Fulhaven. I said no. And that's really why I wanted to talk to you. I said I was alone the whole time, and didn't mention our meeting in that tea-place. I thought it possible they might trace you too to question you. They seem to be very thorough."

"And you want to be sure we tell the same story. I see," said Neil. "For your sake or mine?" he added, watching her.

"For both our sakes," said Caroline. "And you needn't be so sore because I thought you might have been the one who shot Gordon. After all, you thought I was."

His face broke into a genuine smile. "Yes. I'm sorry," he murmured. "I should have known you were not the kind easily turning to violence. But you were a little ambiguous, you know, when you were telling me about finding him in the shelter, and I'm afraid I jumped to the wrong conclusion. I suppose my red hair is partly to blame for your suspicion of me. It does give people a wrong impression till they know me better. But I don't really go about killing men I don't like. I don't even stamp or shout, and as for kicking the cat — " He paused to smile at Colonel who was cleaning his whiskers unconcernedly by the stove. "I think anybody who relieves his feelings that way ought to have his head put in a bucket of water by an absent minded friend who will forget to take it out again."

Caroline relaxed with a faint sigh and smiled, too. "I'm sorry, Neil," she said. "I suppose it *was* partly your hair."

12

"SO now we had better both start thinking again," said Neil, a little later, as they sat in easy chairs in the small sitting-room where Caroline had received him on his first visit. "And I'm not sure that the best thing we can do isn't to tell the police everything we know."

"Oh no! I couldn't!" exclaimed Caroline at once. "The very idea terrifies me. Don't you see, they'd be bound to think I was involved in the murder. I can't even blame them. After all, I went to the very house where he was living and registered there — not in my married name, but as C. Bannister. And I drew attention to myself by looking shocked to death when some woman there said something that made me realize that Gordon was actually Lessing and married to somebody else.

They even got a doctor to take a look at me. Mrs. Lessing's uncle. Then I lied about having a son and about his breaking an arm and dashed off, just after going for a walk in the kind of weather that keeps most people indoors. I couldn't have done more if I'd wanted to be suspected."

"But suppose the police find all that out for themselves, *and* discover that Lessing and Lane are the same person," said Neil, adding a spoonful of brown suggar to his coffee and stirring thoughtfully.

"I can only hope they won't," said Caroline fervently. "I think Gordon must have been very careful not to get his two lives mixed up."

She sipped her own coffee, staring at him anxiously over the rim of her cup, one of a set of blue and gold Crown Derby that had belonged to Aunt Lilian.

"What about his car? Couldn't they find out through that?" asked Neil.

"But why should they bother about

his car?" cried Caroline. "He's been identified as Graham Lessing. Why should they think he was leading a double life? And he always said the car belonged to his firm. I wouldn't be surprised if it was registered and insured in a different name again."

"What about his driving licence?" said Neil.

"He probably had two," said Caroline. "I came across one in the name of Gordon Lane the night before last, when I was looking through his things in search of a clue to his whereabouts."

"If you're right, it would have involved a certain amount of lying and forgery, but I don't suppose that would have worried him," remarked Neil.

"No," agreed Caroline. "But you see why I think we shouldn't go to the police."

"You'll have to explain your husband's protracted absence somehow," he pointed out.

Caroline told him her plan, and he nodded slowly and drank his coffee.

"If you should want to marry again that might pose a bit of a problem," he said, not looking at her. "Officially, you won't be either a divorcee or a widow."

"I shan't want to marry again," she declared, shaking her head.

"That seems waste of good marriagable material," he said, with his faint smile.

She thought to herself that she might say the same thing about him. He seemed unattached and was certainly attractive in his own way. She could not help liking the personality that had emerged during the course of the evening and she was no longer able to see him in her imagination as a killer.

Aloud she remarked: "You're not married, are you, Neil?"

He put down his coffee cup. "Not now," he said quietly. "I was once, but it didn't work. It was one of those things that are fierce while they last but burn themselves out. We might have built something better and more lasting on the ashes, given time, but we were young and she was the impatient type. She found someone else to go mad about while I was fumbling about looking for a formula."

"I'm sorry," murmured Caroline, feeling a new sense of fellowship with him.

"All my own fault, of course," he said almost cheerfully.

"But it doesn't make one's troubles easier to bear to know that," Caroline said wryly, thinking of her own colossal matrimonial blunder.

"I've got over it," he said consolingly, as if he had read her thoughts. "There's a bit of a scar to show where the wound was, but it's scarcely noticeable now. My sister's death hurts a lot more, because I was so sure she was murdered and the murderer seemed to get off scot free. I'm feeling considerably better about that, too, though."

"Do you really think that one murder can cancel out another?" asked Caroline.

"Not exactly," he answered. "I know

that nothing can undo the evil that was done when Rosalind died, but at least her killer can't do any more harm once he, too, is dead. And the fact that he died violently, does, I admit, meet a fundamental desire for justice that not all the intellectual reasoning and humane theorizing in the world can destroy or satisfy."

"But where does justice end and vengeance begin?" asked Caroline doubtfully.

"I suppose each partakes of the nature of the other, to a certain extent," said Neil. "And I don't consider that vengeance is a dirty word. 'Vengeance is mine, saith the Lord.' Doesn't that make it a divine right?"

"Which man shouldn't take upon himself," said Caroline.

"The divine has to work through man," Neil reminded her.

She looked at his grim expression and uneasiness stirred in her again. Was he capable of convincing himself that he was free to kill as an instrument of God?

"Doesn't that quotation go on 'I will repay?'" she said quickly. "I always found that more reassuring, as a child, as if it meant losses would be made good eventually, too."

"Perhaps it does," said Neil. He drank what was left of his coffee and put the cup down.

"Neil," she said earnestly, watching him closely. "Who can have killed Gordon if — " She hesitated.

"If I didn't?" he said, staring back at her.

"As we know we didn't," she corrected him firmly, hiding her fresh doubts.

"It was probably somebody belonging to his life there in Fulhaven," he told her.

"That doctor I mentioned," she said thoughtfully. "He said something to me about being all in favour of surgery — the clean cut. He was talking about matrimonial troubles, really, but he sounded rather ruthless. And he seemed devoted to his niece. Suppose he had just found out what sort of man she was married to."

"You mean *he* might have killed the fellow? Ye-es. A doctor isn't squeamish, but I should have thought he would have used rather more subtle means than shooting him. And he would have needed to possess a gun, which very few people do, you know. Where was the wound, by the way? In the heart or the head, or where?"

"In the chest — near the middle," said Caroline reluctantly. "And — and there was a kind of bloody froth from his mouth," she added, shuddering as she suddenly remembered this detail.

"Through the lungs, then, by the look of it," mused Neil.

"Oh don't," cried Caroline.

"I'm sorry," he said quickly. "I forgot you cared for him."

She shook her head. "It's not that. I'd feel the same about anybody — if I'd seen — "

"Yes. Yes, I'm a clumsy fool. Let's forget it," said Neil remorsefully. "From now on we'll act as if your husband has simply gone off into the blue and you're going to divorce him for desertion."

A gleam came into his eyes. "I wonder if you really could do that," he said. "Bring a divorce action, I mean. It would be undefended, of course, but that would simplify the proceedings."

Caroline stared at him with something like horror. "Bring a divorce action against a dead man?" she cried.

"Why not? It couldn't hurt him," said Neil coolly. He had risen and was walking about the room in a restless manner. "And why should he be considered, anyway?"

"It would be acting a lie — making a mockery of the law," said Caroline.

"Well, what's so sacred about the divorce laws?" asked Neil.

"The law is the law is the law," murmured Caroline. "And I don't think I could go through with it without being found out. I should feel guilty all the time and probably show it."

"Would you?" He stood still and stared at her curiously. "And yet," he said softly, "you have the most inscrutable little face at times. I wondered a good deal what was going on before I first met you."

Disconcerted and rather embarrassed, she said with outward flippancy: "And now you know."

He shook his head. "I'm still wondering," he told her.

They looked at each other in a silence that began to grow tense. The sudden pealing of the front door bell broke the spell. Caroline stared, and glanced at the clock on the mantelpiece. It was ten minutes past nine.

"Who can that be, at this time in the evening?" she said.

"Better go and see," he suggested.

She nodded and murmured: "Excuse me," conventionally.

Less than a week ago, she reflected as she went out of the room, she would not have been half scared to open her own front door, but now she couldn't help a feeling of apprehension at the thought of who might stand beyond it.

This time it was two unknown men, one middleaged and burly, and the other young and slender. But they had oddly similar expressions as they looked at her. The older man, she noticed, was wearing a well cut grey suit, and the young man a sports jacket with drainpipe trousers. Both were hatless, and she could see the lights of a car beyond the gate. She wondered that she had not heard it arrive, but, of course, she and Neil had been in the small sitting-room at the back of the house.

"Mrs. Lane?" said the older man. "Good evening. We are CID officers. Sorry this is rather a late call, but we're making some enquiries and think you might be able to help us. Chief Inspector Smith and Detective Sergeant Low."

Caroline had the feeling that an unpleasant dream was repeating itself, as she glanced at the warrant-card he held out.

"But — but I told the policeman everything I know this afternoon," she protested. "That is, if it's about the murder in Fulhaven last night."

"You said, I believe, that you know nothing at all about it," said Chief Inspector Smith, a little dryly.

"I don't," declared Caroline.

"It *is* about the murder in Fulhaven," said the senior detective with a genial smile that did not quite reach his hard blue eyes.

"Mr. Smith is in charge of the case," said the younger man with respect. "He is from Scotland Yard. I'm local. Do you think we might step inside, Mrs. Lane?"

Caroline hesitated, wondering if she dared refuse them entry, whether, if she did, it would make things look bad for her. Hurriedly she decided that it would.

"Oh, very well," she murmured.

She intended showing them into the drawing-room, but, as they crossed the hall, Neil appeared in the doorway of the small sitting-room, staring out at them, and the Chief Inspector, glimpsing him out of the corner of an eye, turned and greeted him politely.

Neil nodded to him. "Anything the matter?" he asked Caroline, keeping his eyes on the two men.

"These are police officers," she told him woodenly.

"Mr. Lane?" enquired Chief Inspector Smith.

Neil's steady gaze did not falter. "No," he said. "I'm a friend of Mrs. Lane's. My name's Neil Fuller."

"I see. Just keeping her company while her husband is away," remarked Smith with a false geniality.

"She very kindly invited me to dinner tonight," said Neil gravely. "They'd better come in here, hadn't they, my dear?" And he stood aside for them, looking now at Caroline.

"I suppose so," she answered, surprised by the 'my dear' and knowing that he meant something by that glance. Was it a promise of help and support?

The two detectives entered the sitting-room. Their eyes took in the positions of the two coffee cups, which were reasonably far apart in the smallish room, and she guessed what they were doing and why.

"You had better sit down," she murmured ungraciously, dropping down on the sofa she had left to open the door to them. Neil took a seat opposite her as before.

"What we have to say to Mrs. Lane is rather private," said the Chief Inspector meaningly.

"I'd like to hear it all the same," said Neil coolly. "As an old friend, and in the absence of Mr. Lane, I think I ought, eh Caroline?"

"Yes, you'd better stay," she murmured, taking her cue from him.

"Very well," said Smith. "You won't

mind if the officer, here takes a few notes."

"So long as they're accurate, and a true report of what's said, I'm sure Mrs. Lane doesn't mind," said Neil. "Eh, Caroline?"

"No," said Caroline. But she looked at the young man's notebook with some alarm.

The Chief Inspector frowned slightly, then turning away from the intrusive Mr. Fuller, gave his attention to the lady of the house.

"I'm afraid you weren't very frank with the constable who called this afternoon," he said. "For instance, you told him that you didn't know the name Lessing at all. Yet you signed the register at a guesthouse in Fulhaven, which is run by a Mrs. Lessing, only yesterday morning."

Caroline stared at him, momentarily speechless. How had he found out?

"And you didn't put your true name, but the name you write under, Bannister," Smith continued inexorably.

"Why? And why did you add a false address?"

"It was my maiden name — I'd a right to use it," said Caroline. "And the address was my agent's. I — I use that, too, when I don't want to be bothered here at home."

"And did you anticipate being bothered after your trip to Fulhaven yesterday? said Smith, with a slight emphasis on the word 'bothered.'"

"No. At least — I don't know," faltered Caroline.

"Mrs. Lane is too modest to say she was afraid of being pestered by fans," said Neil.

"In that case, why didn't she put her married name in the book?" asked the chief inspector promptly.

Caroline gave Neil a glance of appeal which he received gravely.

"There were special reasons," he said, with an air of reluctance.

"I'm sure there were," said Smith, continuing to stare at Caroline. "For instance, Mrs. Lane, you asked if Mr.

Lane was staying at Regency House when you first called there. You said you were expecting him, yet you were careful *not* to say that *you* were Mrs. Lane."

Caroline glanced at Neil again. "As my friend said, there were special reasons," she said, trying hard to thing of plausible ones, and finding that her usually fertile invention was failing her in this personal crisis.

"Would you care to tell us what they are?" Smith invited, and added not unkindly: "We can be very discreet, you know."

"I'll — I'll think about it," murmured Caroline.

"Yes. Do that," he said. "But there's another question I must ask you — which you are not obliged to answer, of course. Why, having told Mrs. Lessing you intended to stay a night or two, did you suddenly pack and leave that evening, with the excuse that you had telephoned home and found that your small son had broken an arm? Now, according to our information, you have been married for less than a year, and have no children."

Caroline was again speechless, appalled by the extent of his knowledge of her affairs.

"You're quite right, Chief Inspector," said Neil suddenly. "We ought to rely on your discretion." He turned to Caroline, his eyes telling her something — but what? "Darling, will you let me explain?"

His tone of proprietary affection made her blink, but before she could speak he was addressing Smith again.

"In fact, when Mrs. Lane asked at Regency House if Mr. Lane was staying there, she was enquiring not for her husband, but for *me*," he said coolly.

"But your name is Fuller, sir," said the Chief Inspector sharply.

"Yes," said Neil. "But — well, Mrs. Lane thought I might have called myself Lane just — just for the occasion. You see, I had planned to spend a short holiday with her at Fulhaven and she was afraid — well, that I might take advantage of the situation. I'd joked about people taking us for a married couple, and — Anyway, that's why she called herself Bannister. To spike my guns." He gave a rueful little laugh.

Caroline lowered her eyes, not daring to look at him.

"I see, sir," said Smith in an expressionless tone. "But you didn't actually go to Regency House under *any* name, did you?"

"No," said Neil, in the same rueful tone as before. "That's why Caroline rang me in the evening. I'd made a mistake. Thought I wasn't expected till today. She was angry at the mix-up and I'm afraid we had the hell of a row. In the end she said the holiday was off. That's why she rushed away from the guesthouse." He looked at Caroline, his eyes saying: over to you.

"I — I was very upset," she said huskily, secretly shocked by the fluency with which Neil was lying. "I'm afraid

I said the first thing that came into my head, in order to get away at once."

"I know you'll keep this to yourself," added Neil, in a man to man tone. "The fact is, Mrs. Lane isn't happy in her marriage, and she intends to get a divorce as soon as she can."

"I see, sir," said the chief inspector again. "But let me get this clear. You meant to start your holiday together at Regency House today? But there is no booking there for anybody called Fuller *or* Lane."

"I know," said Neil, nodding calmly. "Actually, Mrs. Lane needn't have worried. I never bothered to book at all. Thought it would be easy enough to get in at this time of year."

"You weren't travelling down together?" said Smith, regarding him with narrowed eyes.

"No." Neil glanced at Caroline. "Mrs. Lane had an idea her husband was having her watched, so we thought it better to meet down at Fulhaven, as if by chance."

He stared boldly back at Smith. "I've been telling her, it's lucky, really, we called the whole thing off, with this poor chap, Lessing, getting himself murdered. I take it he was the same Lessing, the proprietor of the guesthouse, I mean."

"It was the husband of the proprietress of Regency House, yes," said Smith. He relaxed and gave a slight nod to the young detective constable, who promptly put away his notebook.

"Well, Mrs. Lane, I'm glad we've got it all sorted out," he said. "It's a pity you weren't more frank with us from the beginning. As I told you, we can be quite discreet. It doesn't do to hide things, when we make an enquiry, you know. We usually find out in the end, and sometimes put the wrong interpretation on things then."

He rose, saying: "Goodbye, Mrs. Lane. Goodbye, sir."

They returned his farewell, politely noticed the detective constable and murmured platitudes. Caroline, all the time, was scarcely able to believe that they were really going, that they were satisfied with Neil's audacious falsehoods.

Then, at the door, the Chief Inspector turned, his shrewd eyes meeting hers and holding her gaze steadily.

"There's just one thing, if I may ask it," he said.

Caroline waited in a resigned despair. She had known they couldn't really get away with it, she and Neil. She had known it in her heart all along.

"If you *could* let me have your autograph for my girl she'd value it greatly, I know," said Smith, with a suddenly very human smile.

13

"I HOPE that can't be called bribery and corruption," remarked Neil, when Caroline came back into the room, after seeing the two police officers out. "An autographed copy of one of your books might be worth something one day."

"After I've figured in a sensational murder trial no doubt," said Caroline, sinking into a chair. She covered her face with her hands. "I can't believe that they've really gone, that they won't be back any minute to ask some more questions."

"I don't think they have any more to ask," said Neil. "If they have we'll have to think up some more answers."

"*You* will," said Caroline, raising her head to look at him. "I don't seem to be very inventive, except on paper. You were quite remarkable, though."

Something in her gaze must have reflected her feelings, which were not entirely admiring, for he made a little grimace.

"You mean I'm a shocking liar," he said. "Will you believe me when I say I'm normally a truthful sort of person, that actually I astonished myself just now by my own performance?"

"You astonished me," murmured Caroline. Then remembering how grateful she ought to be feeling for the help and support he had given her, she added with some warmth: "But I don't know what I should have done without you. Thank you for coming to my rescue so splendidly."

But was it really his own safety he had in mind all along, she wondered. He had claimed, by his story, not to have been in Fulhaven at all yesterday, for instance.

"It was inconsistent of me, as a matter of fact," remarked Neil, "after I'd been saying we ought to tell the police the truth. But I was suddenly afraid."

She looked at him sharply. What was he about to confess? He met the look with an expression in his own eyes she could not quite read.

"You seemed so terribly vulnerable," he said. "I thought Smith was going to charge you any minute and I couldn't bear it. You've been through enough. I wanted to cut you clear of the whole tangle, and I think I succeeded." He gave a sudden engaging grin. "Of course they went away convinced we're lovers, in spite of your virtuous refusal to let me register as your husband at Regency House. But that's given them the satisfaction of finding us guilty of something, though not of murder. So long as they never connect Graham Lessing with Gordon Lane it strengthens our position. But it does cut the ground from under our feet if we do ever want to confess the truth."

"Yes. It would give us such a

motive," murmured Caroline, who had been touched by his admission into feeling a pang of remorse for her suspicion of his motives. "Well, I'd rather be thought an adulterous wife than a murderess."

Then, to her surprise and dismay she felt herself beginning to blush, and once she started she couldn't stop. The warm blood crept up her neck to her face and glowed there for Neil to see. She jumped up quickly.

"I'll make some more coffee. This is cold," she said abruptly, and fled to the kitchen.

She was thankful that he didn't follow, and when she returned, cool and collected, with a pot of fresh coffee, she found him reading one of the books she had brought from her writing-room for Chief Inspector Smith to choose from.

"You write well," he remarked with respect, glancing up. "This is fascinating stuff for kids."

She smiled, aware of a wave of

pleasure at his praise. Gordon, she remembered, had never shown any interest in her actual writings, only in the rewards they won.

"You know," he went on, putting the book down, "it's amazing to me how an intelligent, gifted woman like you could get herself involved with that swine."

"I think it was because my knowledge and experience of real people was so limited," she confessed. "But I'm learning fast," she added dryly. "Soon I shall have got to the stage of trusting nobody at all."

"You can trust me, Caroline," he told her, not protestingly but as if uttering a plain statement of fact.

Their glances met and held each other for a long moment.

"I'll try to accept that, Neil," she murmured, the first to look away.

"Do, please," said Neil. He glanced at his watch. "When I've had another cup of coffee I'll go. I can see you're fagged out. You don't have to tell me

283

you didn't have much sleep last night — if any."

She smiled faintly and admitted that she was tired. Actually she was exhausted suddenly, as if his words had made her realize her state for the first time. She was both glad and sorry that he was going soon. Glad because she wanted to sleep and sleep. Sorry because she wanted company until this blessed slumber arrived — *his* company in particular because he shared with her the knowledge she was afraid might postpone sleep, the awareness of Gordon's death. And that was a secret nobody on earth shared with her but him — except perhaps the murderer.

That thought started up another question in her mind. Was it Gordon Lane who had been murdered or Graham Lessing? Or was it possible that the victim had been neither. Could it have been George Longton who had been shot and killed?

She did not voice this question

284

because of its implications, for who could have a greater grudge against George Longton than Neil himself?

He, too, seemed to have retreated into his own thoughts. They sat and sipped their coffee almost in silence.

When he got up to go she rose, too, and fetched his coat for him and saw him to the door as if he had been any conventional guest departing. She even held out her hand to him at the last. He took it and held it in a firm warm clasp, and then put both hands to it and stood looking down at her as he had done on that first evening when he had appeared, a rather frightening stranger, out of the darkness.

"May I come tomorrow?" he asked. "It won't be till the afternoon, as I've got something on in the morning."

"Yes, come, please," she said.

When he had gone, she stumbled upstairs, with a feeling of having been comforted, and tore off her clothes and tumbled into the bed in the spare room and fell asleep immediately.

She woke wonderfully refreshed, to the sound of church bells and the languid bellowing of cows in a distant field, and lay for a while savouring a feeling of Sabbath calm. But she warned herself that this was probably a period of truce rather than peace. She couldn't hope that all her troubles had been finally settled. She would carry on, however, as if they had.

Soon after breakfast she went into the garden determined to do some work on it. First she would cut the dead blooms from the roses in the front beds.

Ten minutes later, snipping busily away with the secateurs, a Kentish trug at her feet, she paused with an extraordinarily disagreeable sensation before a Queen Elizabeth rose that bore big overblown blooms and had shed some petals as she brushed against it. She saw again, in her imagination, the rose petal lying on the dead man's shoe in the shelter, as her torch had illuminated it. For the first time she began to consider where it could have come from. At the time she had taken it for granted that a freak of the wind had carried it there. But there had been no rosebeds anywhere near. Had somebody dropped it then? And before or after Gordon had died?

She pushed the thought away, telling herself that she had done with such speculation, that it must be left to the police, but it would not have been so easy to dismiss if a voice had not hailed her unexpectedly.

"Don't forget the Harvest Festival's in a fortnight, Mrs. Lane," it said.

Caroline turned and saw that ardent horticulturalist, Mrs. Harding, who had chatted to her in the butcher's shop on the previous Wednesday, when she had been anticipating Gordon's return with such mixed feelings. The large woman had just got out of a particularly small car and was beaming over the gate from under an impressive hat evidently meant for church wear.

"Hard at it I see," she said with

hearty approval. "That azalea wants a bit of nursing if you want to get the best out of it next spring. Hope you haven't been giving it tap water. I thought Mr. Lane would be mowing the lawn this morning, as he isn't one of the church goers and doesn't play golf. Or is he cleaning his car?"

She gave a guffaw of laughter, to show that this was a joke. But Caroline looked at her unsmilingly.

"My husband is away," she said in reserved tones.

"Oh, but I thought — " began Mrs. Harding, and gave her a puzzled stare.

Caroline remembered that their previous conversation had run on very similar lines. What was it Mrs. Harding had thought about Gordon? She did not ask the question aloud, but her eyes were full of enquiry now, and Mrs. Harding answered them.

"I thought he must have been coming home when I saw him on Tuesday," she said. "I was surprised when you said on Wednesday that you were expecting him. Did he pop off again immediately? He does get about, doesn't he!"

"You saw my husband here in Oxridge last Tuesday," exclaimed Caroline. "At what time?"

"Why, in the morning," said Mrs. Harding, looking puzzled again. "I had just passed here on my way to the shops. You had a visitor leaving, I remember, a young man with red hair. Then, a little farther on, Mr. Lane passed me, driving this way. I waved, and he waved back. Naturally, I thought he was coming home. Oh dear! I hope I haven't said anything indiscreet."

Caroline gathered her wits together.

"No. Don't worry, Mrs. Harding," she said. "But I know you will understand, when I say I don't want to talk about my husband's coming and goings at the moment. It's rather a painful subject."

"Oh dear!" exclaimed Mrs. Harding again, looking interested, concerned and embarrassed in quick succession. "I shouldn't have dreamed of mentioning it if I'd known. I do hope things will be better soon."

Caroline merely shook her head. Then she said, with an air of intentionally changing the subject: "Thank you for reminding me of the Harvest Festival."

"It's in a fortnight. I think I told you," said Mrs. Harding, evidently relieved to be back on safe conversational ground. "We mustn't rob you of your dahlias — you haven't many this year, have you. But michaelmas daisies always make good background material. And do I see some Worcesters still hanging in your little orchard at the back? They'll be woolly eating by then but very decorative. But I mustn't be late for church. How nice you look in slacks. I only wish I could wear 'em. But I haven't the figure."

With a hurried farewell, she bundled into the small car, waved and drove away, leaving Caroline to digest the startling information she had given her.

Gordon had returned on Tuesday, a day earlier than he had planned, and had driven away again almost immediately after Mrs. Harding had seen him. What had happened was clear. He had seen Neil coming away from Willow Lodge and recognized him. What had he thought? That he was totally exposed to her and would have to make a permanent retreat from the situation? Or was he intending merely to lie low for a while?

Caroline wondered what excuse he had given his beautiful, placid wife for his sudden return to Fulhaven, and whether she had believed him. And what of the shrewd eyed old doctor? Suppose he had begun to suspect that Gordon was playing a double game of some sort, how much would he have resented it on behalf of his niece? To the point of murder? It didn't seem likely. Unless he already hated Gordon, and this was the last straw.

Neil had thought the shooting out of character for a doctor, but couldn't this have been a deliberate bluff — to draw away any suspicion that might be directed against himself? Or had his hatred been so violent that a crude killing seemed natural?

Caroline shivered in spite of the warm day, feeling again some of the horror she had experienced at the scene of the crime. She had planned going through Gordon's belongings again to make sure there was nothing to tie him to his Fulhaven identity, but felt she must revive herself with coffee first.

She was in the kitchen when the front door bell rang. Her heart seemed to somersault as she thought that it might be the police come to question her again, this time without Neil's supporting presence. But could it be Neil himself, arrived earlier than he had expected?

She patted her hair and took a quick glance in the mirror with the heavy gilded frame that hung in the hall, as she passed it. She looked slim and rather elegant in her dark blue slacks and over-blouse of thick gaily patterned cotton, and her pale face with the faintly slanting eyes had the fragility of an old Chinese painting. She was very nervous, but she was surprised to see that her expression showed nothing of this emotion. Well, thank goodness for an old-fashioned upbringing that had schooled her in self control, she thought as she went on to open the door.

In spite of this, she gave a start of surprise at sight of her caller, a middle-aged man with melancholy brown eyes, wearing a half-opened rose in the lapel of his good grey suit.

At the first instant of seeing him she thought: 'Who is it? Somebody I've met only recently.' Then she remembered the office in Holborn, up the steep dark stairs.

"Mr. Dobson!" she exclaimed. "This is a surprise. How did you know where I live?"

"I hope you don't mind my calling like this, Mrs. Lane," he said anxiously. "You dropped an envelope when you were in my office, if you'll remember, the envelope containing the photograph you showed me. It had your address on it. I couldn't help noticing. I've got the kind of mind that marks and remembers that sort of thing. It's partly training, I suppose, dealing with so many different people in my work, some of them foreign with difficult names and living in odd places."

"Yes, I see," said Caroline. "You'd better come in."

But she eyed him a little as though he carried an explosive somewhere about him, for she felt sure that he came with more information about Gordon and that she was probably not going to like it.

He confirmed this suspicion right away, as he stepped into the hall, by saying: "But I shouldn't boast of my memory, because I'm afraid it wasn't functioning very well when you came

294

to see me last Tuesday. At least — "

He broke off, as she showed him into the seldom used drawing-room, and said in a different tone: "You have a charming place here, Mrs. Lane, and quite secluded. I have a house a little way out of London myself, but in Surrey, not Kent. My garden isn't as big as yours, but I go in for greenhouses. I'm very fond of flowers.

"Yes," said Caroline, with a glance at the rose in his coat, which gave her an oddly mixed feeling of attraction and repulsion. "Won't you sit down."

She waited till they had both seated themselves in large armchairs a little distance apart before she asked: "Is there something you've remembered about — about my husband?"

Mr. Dobson nodded uneasily. "He isn't at home, I take it," he murmured, looking round the room almost as if he feared Gordon might be hiding behind the curtains or the large Chesterfield.

"No," said Caroline. "He hasn't come back. I may as well tell you.

I think he has gone for good."

"Oh. Really?" exclaimed Mr. Dobson, looking startled. "You hadn't anticipated that when you came to see me, had you?"

Caroline shook her head and told herself she must be careful. And she had to appear surprised when he told her about Gordon having been Longton — which was what he was going to do, she felt sure.

"Perhaps I didn't want to admit it even to myself," she said, with an air of profundity.

He stared at her, murmuring: "Very natural." Then he said more briskly: "Well, the fact is I did really have a feeling the face was somehow familiar when you showed me that snap of your husband. But I couldn't put a name to it. I didn't believe I'd ever actually met your husband, only seen somebody very like him somewhere, and at some time. Then, after you had gone, it came back to me, and I realized that I *had* known him. Only, when I knew him he was wearing a beard and calling himself by a different name."

"Oh?" said Caroline. "How — how extraordinary!"

"Yes," nodded Dobson, fixing her with his melancholy stare. "It was as John Brown that I knew him — up in Glasgow. I met him from time to time when I went to Scotland on business — Oh, five or six years ago it must be. We patronized the same pub and played golf together once or twice. But I haven't seen him since then. I stopped going about so much myself, you see."

"Brown?" repeated Caroline, astonished. "John Brown? But — " She checked herself. "It doesn't seem possible," she ended weakly. Confused, she wondered if Brown could be yet another alias of Gordon's. Then she saw that this would still leave unexplained the problem of why Mr. Dobson, having remembered the beard, didn't also remember that John Brown was identical with the George Longton who had married his secretary, Rosalind Fuller. According to Neil, he had been to the wedding. Not to have recognized Gordon in the photograph at all would have been understandable considering the change in his appearance and the lapse of time, but to identify him wrongly and to come all this way on a Sunday morning to do it, was not. It was strange and disturbing.

14

MR. DOBSON leaned back in his chair with the little sigh of one who has successfully carried out a painful task.

"I'm afraid there isn't any more I can tell you," he said. "It was quite a long time ago. You'd have a job to make a connection now. John Brown is a common enough name, and I can give you very few details."

"Yes," said Caroline. "I see that."

"I suppose it's possible that your husband has assumed this other identity again — or may never actually have discarded it," Dobson continued thoughtfully.

Caroline gulped and clenched her hands, as she was assailed by a sudden vision of Gordon dead in the shelter.

"I'm sorry if the idea upsets you," exclaimed Mr. Dobson, looking anxious again. "But you did seem resigned to the belief that he was not coming back to you."

"Yes," said Caroline again. "It's all right."

"It's not for me to give you advice, of course," continued her visitor, his melancholy brown eyes fixed unblinkingly on her. "But it might be better to try to forget all about him, in the circumstances."

She nodded. "I think so, too, Mr. Dobson," she assured him.

She wanted to think about what he had said, but she didn't want him to go yet.

"Thank you very much for coming," she said. "I was just going to make myself some coffee. Please stay and have a cup with me."

"It's very kind of you. Thank you," he said, evidently relieved now. "I'm so glad you've taken my news so well. I was rather worried."

She wondered whether she had taken it a little too well. But she gave him a faint smile and hurried from the room, murmuring excuses.

Her mind was secretly in a turmoil. Why had he lied? Why? And come here specially to do it, as if it was of great importance? There was an answer waiting, but it seemed too monstrous to be admitted. Yet if she did acknowledge it so many things would fall into place. For instance, there was the detective agency she had noticed sharing the premises in Holborn with Dobson and Perks.

Suppose when she left there on Tuesday Dobson had gone into them and said she was to be followed on his behalf. Not right away. There wouldn't have been time for that. But she knew now that he had memorized her address. So could he be responsible for the motor-cyclist who had dogged her way ever since she had glimpsed him watching the garden from behind the screen of willows? Was it Dobson he had been ringing from the call-box in Fulhaven on Friday? To say what?

That he had tracked her there, but that she had challenged him and seemed suspicious of him, so it wouldn't do for him to continue his tailing of her? And then what?

Caroline paused with a spoonful of coffee poised over the percolator, and stared with glazed eyes. Suppose Dobson himself had taken over and driven fast down to Fulhaven and suppose he had been given the number of her car and recognized it along by the Promenade, and gone walking along there in search of her and met Gordon instead — Gordon, who had been his real quarry all along!

Had he been wearing a flower in his coat, as usual? A pink rose perhaps? And had he come armed with a gun — a small revolver perhaps that would go in a raincoat pocket?

Half the coffee went into the percolator, the rest spilled over the stove, as her hand trembled suddenly.

If her ideas were right then the murder had been premeditated, and

Dobson was the man who had done it. A murderer was sitting calmly in her drawing-room, waiting for her to bring him coffee. And he seemed so ordinary!

She spilled a second spoonful of coffee as she heard him calling her name. Conquering her fear and repugnance with an effort, and telling herself that she must not let him see how she felt, she went out of the kitchen and into the hall with a good show of composure, though her heart was beating much too fast and she had to control her breathing. He was standing outside the drawing-room door.

"I'm sorry, Mrs. Lane. I find I can't stay for coffee after all," he said, quickly. "I've just remembered another call I must make before lunch."

She did not believe in his excuse, but she accepted it graciously and escorted him to the front door, secretly wondering if he had taken advantage of her absence in the kitchen to have a quick look round for some purpose of his own.

When she had seen him get into a big fat foreign looking car at the gate, she shut the door and hurried into the drawing-room and stared at the armchair he had sat in with a wondering horror, as if the slight depression in the cushion was the imprint of the devil himself. But everything else in the room seemed undisturbed.

It was nearly three o'clock when Neil came. Caroline, who had been listening for his car, hurried to open the door and watched with a feeling of comfort and relief, his tall figure get out. The sun made a fiery halo of his hair. It was strange how familiar his appearance had become to her in such a short space of time. She knew so well, she felt, the hairs at the back of his neck that glinted like metal threads when he turned his head to shut the car door: the way his reddish brows drew together in that little frown of his when he was startled or surprised:

his long legged, easy stride.

He smiled warmly, when he saw her waiting so hospitably for him with the door open. Then he frowned.

"More trouble?" he said softly, when he had reached her. "What is it? Have the police been here again?"

She shook her head. "No," she said, then blurted: "I've had another sort of visitor — Mr. Dobson of Dobson and Perks."

"What?" he exclaimed, the frown deepening. "How did he know where you lived? What did he want?"

She took him into the sitting-room before answering and shut the door as if there might be the danger of eavesdroppers creeping about the quiet house. She tried to be calm and factual as she recounted what had been said in that surprising interview, and Neil listened with an air of puzzled incredulity.

"Brown? John Brown? What on earth was he talking about?"

"Yes, what?" she said meaningly.

"And, Neil, I've had an idea — several, in fact. I told you I was followed to Fulhaven by that motor-cyclist who was hanging about the Hand in Hand. Well, there's a detective agency in the same building as Dobson's offices, and he got my address from an envelope I had dropped. I think he had that tail put on me."

There was no doubt Neil was interested. His tawny eyes never left hers, as she talked. But he still had an air of puzzlement.

"But why would Dobson do a thing like that?" he asked slowly.

"To find Gordon, of course," she answered a little impatiently. "In the hope I would lead the way to him. After all, *you* took some pains to track Gordon down after you'd seen him again by chance."

"Yes, but Dobson wouldn't have had my reasons," Neil protested. "At least — " he broke off. "No, it's impossible!" he muttered.

"Well, I don't think it is," Caroline

306

maintained. "There's just one thing. How well did Dobson know you, actually? Because if that motor-cyclist was reporting all my movements to his employer he must have mentioned my meeting with you at the Hand in Hand, and your red hair is rather distinctive. Would Dobson have guessed who you are? If so he could be sure you'd told me about Gordon having been George Longton."

"We only met once, as a matter fact, and that was at the wedding," answered Neil. "I doubt if he took much notice of me then. According to my mother, he had eyes only for the bride."

"Then he probably came this morning imagining I didn't know a thing about Gordon's past," said Caroline.

"You didn't throw any doubt on his story, did you? Or hint that you knew better?" asked Neil.

"Oh no," said Caroline. "I was terribly taken aback, but he seemed to think that quite natural."

"Yes, I suppose he would," said Neil.

"But I still can't believe he had you followed, Caroline."

"Well, somebody did," said Caroline, a shade defiantly. "And I'm pretty sure now that it was Dobson." She hesitated, then went on in a similar tone. "What's more I think he drove to Fulhaven himself when his man rang him to say I'd seen through him, and I think he met Gordon in that shelter and shot him."

She expected Neil to protest, but he merely shook his head and looked doubtful, then said almost pityingly: "You haven't the smallest evidence, really, you know. I suppose you're simply guessing — or do you call it intuition?"

"I call it reason and common-sense plus a little imagination, declared Caroline tartly. "There's another thing. Didn't you say Dobson always wore a flower in his jacket?"

"He did six years ago, according to Rosalind," said Neil, with a slight shrug.

"He was wearing a rose last Tuesday, and another this morning," Caroline told him. "And there was a single rosepetal clinging to one of Gordon's shoes when I found him. I can't see that it *could* have blown all the way from those flowerbeds in front of the Majestic and the Grand Hotel, and there aren't any others. But it could have been dropped by somebody bending over him — to make sure that he was dead, for instance."

"Yes," Neil admitted, "I suppose it could. But did you ever walk on beyond that last shelter? There's a cottage down there, tucked away rather, but with a fine show of roses round the door, and the wind *was* blowing from that direction."

"Oh," said Caroline. "I didn't know." She was a little shaken.

"Besides, why should Dobson want to kill Longton?" Neil went on. "As far as I know, they were the merest acquaintances."

"You said just now he had eyes only

for your sister," Caroline reminded him. "Did you mean he was attracted by her?"

Neil shrugged. "My mother thought he was keen on her, but too much the woman-shy bachelor to take the plunge."

"Well, there you are!" exclaimed Caroline. "There's your motive, jealousy and frustration, plus a desire to revenge your sister."

"But as far as he was aware, Rosalind's death was reported as an accident," Neil protested. "I never shared my suspicions with Dobson, I can assure you. And, anyway, as I said when you were inclined to suspect me, a man's emotions don't stay red hot for five or six years."

"He could be the type of man who broods and broods until he gets an obsession," said Caroline. "And if he's so innocent, why did he tell me that lie about Gordon having been called John Brown?"

Neil smiled. "What makes you so

sure it was a lie?" he asked.

"You're not suggesting it was true!" cried Caroline incredulously. "That he was Longton *and* Brown?"

"No. But Dobson might have spoken in good faith," said Neil. "If he just thought the photograph you showed him was vaguely familiar but couldn't remember where he'd seen a face like it, and afterwards thought of some fellow named Brown he used to know in Scotland about the same time as he knew Longton and who bore a superficial resemblance to him, he might have made a genuine mistake. You might be right in your idea about his feelings for Rosalind, but it's possible it would affect him in the opposite way to the one you imagine — make him shrink from thinking of Longton, I mean, because of reviving too painful memories. In which case his subconscious mind might have pounced on John Brown as an easy way out."

"Psychology in one easy lesson!" murmured Caroline naughtily. "I'm afraid I find that all a bit far fetched."

"As I find your so-called evidence," said Neil.

They looked at each other with something like hostility, and Caroline realized that they were on the verge of quarrelling.

"We'd better agree to differ," she said with a smile. "But please explain why Dobson had me followed."

"The explanation is that he didn't," said Neil, with a smile as pleasant as her own.

"Oh, I see. You think I imagined it all?" said Caroline, determined to keep her temper, but speaking gently with some difficulty.

"No no," he said quickly. "But I think the fact that a detective agency shares the same building as Dobson and Perks could be no more than a coincidence. There's nothing to say that Dobson ever patronized it, is there?"

"If he wasn't responsible for that

motor-cyclist's antics, then who was?" asked Caroline.

He looked out of the window as he answered quietly: "Who's the most likely person to have a woman watched and followed, after all?" Then his glance met hers again. "Her husband, surely."

15

CAROLINE stared at him, remembering that this had been her reaction, when she first suspected she was being tailed.

"Actually I thought of that right away but dismissed the idea," she admitted half reluctantly. "But there's something I haven't told you yet. If Gordon saw you leaving here and recognized you he just might have had me followed to see what I would do."

Neil was frowning in bewilderment. "What are you talking about?" he asked. "When could Longton have seen me leaving here?"

"On Tuesday morning," said Caroline. "I was coming to it, but telling you about Dobson's visit seemed more important." She went on to recount her conversation with Mrs. Harding. "It explains why Gordon didn't come home on Wednesday and never wrote or phoned to say why," she ended.

"It certainly does. It explains a great deal, in fact," said Neil. "The question is, did he go straight back to Fulhaven, or to London, where it would be easier to get hold of a private investigator?"

"I don't know," said Caroline. "I only know he was in Fulhaven by Friday morning."

Neil was looking at her oddly with a flicker of anxiety in his tawny eyes. "There's another question, Caroline — a very important one," he said.

"What is it?" she asked, catching the hint of trouble from him and showing it now in her own eyes.

"Did he approach the detective agency in the name of Lane or Lessing?" said Neil. "Because if it was Lessing, I'm afraid you could really be in the soup."

"You mean they could get in touch with the police and tell them? Oh no!" gasped Caroline. "That would be too awful! It would give them the means of tracing Graham Lessing right to this doorstep, and they'd soon discover he was Gordon Lane, too."

And then her lies and evasions would seem like the desperate attempts of the guilty to escape justice, she thought, with rising panic. Of course they would suspect her of the murder. Opportunity, motive — more than one motive if they thought Neil was her lover — plus the fact, underlined by Mrs. Hedges, that the police always went for the wife or husband of a victim first.

"I didn't mean to frighten you, Caroline," said Neil with contrition, reading something of her feelings in her startled stare. "But I thought you ought to realize the danger. I expect, after all, that he would have given the name, Lane, in the circumstances. If he went to a respectable agency they might want to know why he wanted another man's wife followed, if he'd said he was Lessing. Whereas there wouldn't be any need for a man to give a reason for having a tail put on his own wife.

Naturally it would be assumed that it was a preliminary to a divorce action."

Caroline saw the truth of this and relaxed slightly. "Oh, you really had me scared," she sighed, Then she gave a little smile. "But I'm glad I needn't think of Mr. Dobson as a murderer any more. I was quite certain of his guilt, you know, till you talked me out of it. You've missed your vocation. You ought to be a barrister — counsel for the defence."

It suddenly occurred to her that she was in no position to talk about his missing a vocation. She had no idea what he did for a living.

"Of course, I don't know that you're *not* a barrister," she remarked. "You've told me so little about yourself."

He shrugged. "There's so little to tell. But I'm certainly not a barrister. A humble accountant, that's me."

"Oh well, I suppose that means you have a logical mind," said Caroline. "I think people who deal in figures are very brainy."

"And I think people who write junior historical novels are," said Neil with a smile. "They have a lot more imagination, too."

"And — don't tell me — imagination can be a dangerous quality," murmured Caroline, rising.

She knew a little more about him now, she was thinking. But she wanted to know more.

"You had Friday off from the office, then," she said.

"I work for myself," he told her, "and can always make time up in the evening. That's what I did after I'd met you, as a matter of fact, I drove home and put in a couple of hours work."

"You live with your mother, don't you?" she went on, probing cautiously.

"With both my parents," he answered. "At least, I have rooms at the top of their big old house. It's convenient and pleases them."

He stood looking down at her a little quizzically, then he said softly: "Well? Shall we go?"

"Go?" She was startled. "Go where?"

"I'm taking you out," he told her. "I thought that was the understanding. And let's try to forget murder and bigamy for the time being, shall we?"

"Oh, if I could!" she sighed.

"Perhaps it will be easier for me," he murmured, with a lingering look at her shining dark hair and petite figure. "You're so pretty."

The compliment surprised and pleased her. In the past she would not have known what to do with it. Now she smiled and thanked him quite naturally.

"And amazingly tough," he added disconcertingly.

Then she saw that he meant this for a compliment, too. And wasn't it true? Wouldn't a more sensitive woman be half demented by now with the shock upon shock she had endured. But all the time she had experienced this strange feeling that it was all happening outside her real life, a life that Gordon himself had never actually penetrated into.

She was very quiet, sitting beside Neil in the car, letting him drive her where he chose through the gentle, still green countryside, avoiding the main roads and the routes to the coast. He stopped the car once to let them look at a view of undulating fields with cattle grazing in them peacefully and flocks of birds rising and falling as they fed in the golden stubble the harvested corn had left behind.

He drew up again another time along a lane that ran through a pine wood, and they watched a squirrel eating a cone, turning it round and round in his small paws and nibbling furiously.

They had tea in a charming village, where parking wasn't easy and Sunday traffic disturbed the Sabbath peace, but where the church tower had stood for eight hundred years and the churchyard yew for nearly as long, and the tea-room had oak beams in its ceiling that had been darkening there since the fifteenth century.

Later they walked for a while

beside a placid river, watching the couples boating and the family parties picknicking, the happy dogs and the staring infants, the small boys fishing for minnows.

When Neil took her hand and held it as they strolled, Caroline made no objection. They walked united by their silence, too, and cut off — or so she imagined — from all the carefree people about them by the sinister knowledge they shared.

"A penny for them," said Neil suddenly.

Caroline gave a shrug and a rueful smile. "I agreed to try and forget my troubles," she said, "but whatever line of thought I follow seems to lead back to them. Somehow, though, they don't seem so terrible out here in the sunshine, with everybody bent on enjoying himself. And there's always something soothing about a quietly flowing river."

"Especially when there are swans," remarked Neil, as a couple of these great white birds sailed majestically into sight.

"I like September," he murmured, gazing from them to where rounded white clouds sailed with equal grace in the soft blue sky.

It was last September that she had first met Gordon, Caroline remembered. If she had not gone to that hotel in Scarborough — But it was no good going over the past, wondering if she had been a predestined victim, or just an innocent fool who might have avoided disaster by exercising a little wisdom. She might as well imagine how different Gordon's fate would have been if *he* had not gone to Scarborough or picked on her hotel for tea that afternoon. Perhaps he would not now be lying dead in some mortuary. Or wouldn't it have made any difference? From which of his lives had his murderer come?

"Neil," she said. "I wonder what Gordon was really doing between the time of your sister's death and his meeting with me a year ago."

"Doing?" repeated Neil vaguely. "Didn't you say he had been married to the Lessing woman for ten years."

"Yes," said Caroline. "But with frequent absences according to Dr Hardwick. I'm wondering just how long some of those absences were. I mean did he actually live for a time in South America, as he told me?"

Neil released her hand in order to pluck a handful of grass to throw to the swans, who bent their long white necks gracefully to snap their beaks at it.

"Why should it matter?" he asked.

"Don't you see? I'm wondering if there was yet another woman in his life," said Caroline. "Perhaps he had a fourth wife somewhere. I can see now that he lived off women. If he committed bigamy twice, why not three or four, or even five times, in fact?"

"It's possible, yes," murmured Neil, still watching the swans. "But I think myself, he would have wanted spells of freedom in order to spend the money he got from his victims. I mean, why go to all the trouble he did in order to live a humdrum existence in a guesthouse at Fulhaven? No, my bet is he was leading a third life of secret luxury somewhere."

Caroline had to acknowledge that he could well be right. "But it still means he had another identity we know nothing about," she pointed out. It gives us a wider field in which to look for his killer."

He glanced at her quickly, then away again. "*We* don't have to look for his killer, thank God!" he said. "Personally my sympathies rather lie with him, anyway."

"Yet you wanted me to tell the police everything," Caroline reminded him.

"That was for your own sake," he told her, and added abruptly: "Let's go back to the car."

As they returned the way they had come, past the boaters and the pushchairs and the dogs and the small fishermen, Caroline murmured: "Do

324

you think he truly cared for her — his real wife? She's beautiful in her own way."

Neil shrugged. "I'd say he never cared for anybody except himself. But everybody needs an anchorage of some sort. She was probably no more than that to him." Then, looking straight ahead, he asked: "Do you mind terribly, Caroline?"

She shook her head. "Whatever love I had for Gordon was dead before he was," she said honestly.

"I'm glad of that," he murmured.

She did not remind him that he himself had helped in that killing. They continued their walk to the car in silence. When they had reached it he glanced at his watch and seemed to hesitate.

"I'm afraid I've got to get back now," he said. "I've a long standing engagement this evening that can't be put off. Sorry."

She felt acutely disappointed, realizing how much she had counted on his company for the rest of the evening. There was a certain constraint in his manner, too, that made her wonder if she had offended him.

"Of course you must keep your engagement," she said. "Thank you for taking me out. I've enjoyed it." Her tone was polite and formal.

They were almost strangers again, it seemed to her, as they drove back to Willow Lodge.

"Would you like me to come in with you, just to make sure everything is all right?" Neil offered, when they got there.

"No need for that," she told him, seeing him glance at his watch again. "*I'm* not in any danger, you know."

"I suppose not," he muttered. "But ring me, if you're in any sort of trouble. You have my number."

She nodded and thanked him, forbearing to ask him what good that was if he was going off again immediately he got home. She paused at her gate, to wave him a brief goodbye, before going up the drive to the lonely house.

But she was not quite forsaken. Colonel was there in the porch, and very glad to see her, to judge by his loud greeting. Well, even the affection and companionship of a cat was not to be sneezed at, she thought as she unlocked the door and they went in together. And, after all, she had never minded being alone for quite long periods in the past. Her best work had been done at such times. And there were old friends she could invite to visit her now. Mary Green would be home soon.

One thing she knew. She would not rely on seeing much of Neil Fuller. She had made a fool of herself once over a man and she dared not trust too easily again. Had he invented that engagement for this evening? Or was it something very special and private? A date with his best girl, perhaps? Well, it was nothing to her. But he had been kind. That was something she could see now that Gordon had never been. Seductive, exciting, flattering at times, but not kind.

She gave Colonel his supper and had her own meal from a tray in front of the television set. The noise of it drowned the creaks and rustles which seemed to haunt the old house at night, as the wind got up after sunset, and once or twice she actually forgot the happenings of the last few days and lost herself for a while in the screen shadows.

She was in the bathroom, preparing for bed, when the phone rang, sending an absurd tremor of apprehension through her. She ran downstairs to the instrument in the hall rather than take the call on the extension in the matrimonial bedroom.

"Hallo," she said breathlessly.

"It's me, Neil Fuller," said Neil's voice against a background of voices and a faint clink of glasses. "I wanted to make sure everything was all right."

"Yes, thank you," she assured him. "I'm just going to bed."

"Sleep tight, Caroline," he said softly. "Goodnight." There was a sound as though somebody had drawn a bow across the strings of a violin, making a sharp discord, then a ripple of laughter, and the line went dead.

Where had he been phoning from, she wondered. Was there some sort of party on wherever it was? But she was grateful to him for ringing, and still felt the comfort of it when she woke from time to time through the long night.

Monday was one of Mrs. Hedges's mornings. She spent most of the time at the washing-machine, singing mournful hymns to the accompanyment of its drone. She came into the kitchen carrying her usual shopping basket, as Caroline was washing up her few breakfast dishes.

"Good morning, Mrs. Lane," she said, eyeing the evidence of her employer's solitary meal. "Mr. Lane still not back?"

Although she had been expecting this

enquiry, a sense of guilt made Caroline stiffen.

"No," she said, in a tone that was not quite natural, "No, he isn't."

She had risen early that morning with the determination, once more, to try and carry on as usual, and had actually put in an hour's work on her book before breakfast, though she had sat in front of the typewriter for some time before she could concentrate sufficiently to do any actual writing.

Mrs. Hedges continued to stare, while she unbuttoned her coat and took it off.

"There's nothing wrong, is there, Mrs. Lane?" she asked. "You look a bit poorly still, if you ask me." She gave a quick glance at Caroline's slim figure, speculation in the look again.

Caroline seized her chance. "You're quite an old friend really, Mrs. Hedges," she said. "I know I can trust you."

Mrs. Hedges paused at the peg where she was hanging her coat and looked round with popping eyes. "Yes," she breathed. "Oh yes."

"The fact is, my husband is not coming back at all," Caroline declared bluntly. "He has left me."

Mrs. Hedges's face became violently suffused under the crocheted pudding basin hat which she had not yet taken off.

"He never!" she exclaimed dramatically. "Don't tell me there's another woman — and you two married not a twelve month!"

"Yes, I'm afraid there is," said Caroline, thinking of Mrs. Lessing. "Perhaps more than one."

"Go on! A proper little Henry the Eighth!" said Mrs. Hedges, indignantly. "Only, *he* did have 'em one at a time. Well, I always did say you was too good for him, Mrs. Lane. It's his loss, what he's done. Not yours. And I hope she'll turn out one of them proper bitches, whoever she is — if you'll pardon the language. I hope all of 'em do. That'll teach him to desert a nice tempered young lady like you, that's a pleasure to work for."

Caroline could not help a smile, which her henchwoman fortunately took for one of appreciation rather than amusement. It was so clear that Mrs. Hedges, although truly sympathetic and partisan, was enjoying the situation very much.

"I know you'll understand that I don't want to talk about it," said Caroline. "It's been rather a shock, finding all this out."

"Course it has," said Mrs. Hedges. "No wonder you look poorly. Wouldn't you like to have a nice lie-down, while I get on with everything?"

"No thank you," Caroline answered. "I hope to carry on as usual."

"Well, I think you're ever so brave, Mrs. Lane," remarked the other woman. "But mind you don't collapse all of a sudden. It's what my niece, Greta did, when she was jilted three days before the wedding."

"I shall be all right," said Caroline,

wondering what Mrs. Hedges would say if she knew the actual truth, if she were to tell her that Gordon had been a liar, a bigamist, possibly a murderer, and that he had just been murdered himself. She would probably think her employer had gone mad. Murder was only something that happened in newspapers and paperbacks.

With the thought, Caroline glanced down at the Daily Mirror that Mrs. Hedges, still forgetful of her hat, had taken out of her shopping bag and placed upon the table while she fished for her slippers in the same receptacle. There, facing her, was Gordon himself, or rather his photograph.

'Found Shot in Shelter' screamed the headline above it. 'The murdered man, Mr. G. Lessing,' said the caption beneath.

Caroline heard her blood singing in her head, a mist began to form at the edges of her vision as she stared at the newspaper, unable to wrench her gaze away.

"Oh dear! Sit down, dear. Put your head between your legs," said Mrs. Hedges's voice from far away, and she felt herself guided to a chair and placed in it, then her head being pushed down by large, capable hands.

The faintness passed, leaving only a desperate feeling of anxiety.

"You sit quiet for a bit, Mrs. Lane," said the daily. "I knew you wasn't feeling as well as you pretended. And I expect that picture give you a nasty shock. I ought to have warned you."

"W — warned me?" faltered Caroline.

"That it was a bit like Mr. Lane," said Mrs. Hedges. "Older, though I should say. Looks as if the poor chap had grey hair, not fair. But naturally it reminded you. Brought it all back, like."

"Yes. Yes, that's just how it was," murmured Caroline, marvelling that her henchwoman couldn't see that it was Gordon himself staring up at them from the printed page. Not that it was a good photograph. In fact, it looked as if it was blown up from a rather poorly taken, over exposed amateur effort.

"What about a drop of brandy? Or shall I make you a nice cup of tea?" said Mrs. Hedges solicitously.

"Brandy, I think. But I'll get it myself. Don't you bother," said Caroline, rising. "I'm feeling better already."

Perhaps, she thought — as she lay, with strength and courage slowly returning, on the sofa in the small sitting-room, and raised her head from time to time to take small sips of the brandy — perhaps the publication of that photograph was not really so catastrophic. Nobody knew Gordon intimately in Oxridge. In fact, Mrs. Hedges had seen more of him than anybody, and if she had not recognized him just now then the chances were nobody else would. People largely saw what they expected to see, too, and who would expect to see a portrait of Mr. Lane of Oxridge printed as that of Mr. Lessing of Fulhaven, a victim of murder?

There was only Mr. Dobson to worry about. If he should see the thing and recognize it, and link it up with what she had told him of her husband being missing, then he might possibly go to the police. But it was unlikely that he would be a reader of the Daily Mirror. There had been only an unillustrated paragraph dealing with the case in her own Times, for instance.

Neil, too, would probably not have seen it. Perhaps she ought to do something about that. She sat up, swung her legs round and stood up, a little too quickly. Overcoming a slight feeling of giddiness, she went to her writing-room and shut the door, having heard from the hall the sound of Mrs. Hedges singing 'A few more Years Shall Roll,' as she ran water into the washing machine.

She got through to Neil at once.

"Have you seen the Mirror this morning?" she asked.

"No. The Telegraph and the Financial Times, that's all," he answered. "Why?"

"I think you should," she said cautiously.

After a slight pause, he said: "Yes, I'll do that. Something interesting?"

"Very. It hasn't had any repercussions yet, but one never knows. I expect you're busy, so I won't keep you. I wouldn't have rung if it hadn't been quite important."

"I see," he said quietly, and she was sure he had understood.

When she had replaced the receiver she lingered, elbows on desk and chin on hands, wondering why she imagined Neil should concern himself, after all. If he had been speaking the truth when he told her he was not even in Fulhaven on Friday night when Gordon had been killed, the publication of the photograph was no danger to him. But hadn't he involved himself when he had hinted at a love affair with her to those two detectives? Perhaps he was wishing now that he had never set eyes on her. In any case, he probably despised her a little, secretly, for falling so readily for the spurious charm of the man he had hated.

She told herself that work was the antidote to these depressing thoughts. She must try to be glad of her recovered independence and get down to her book again.

She tried, after she had made a brief journey to the shops in her car, but it was very hard to concentrate. By eleven o'clock she had achieved only a couple of paragraphs that she had not crossed out, and it was time for coffee.

At half past twelve Mrs. Hedges appeared in the doorway. "I'm off now, Mrs. Lane," she said. "Just got to get me hat and coat on." She added: "All that washing on the line has been through the spin-dryer, so keep an eye on the weather, won't you."

Caroline, who had been lost in an unhappy reverie that had nothing to do with her craft, said vaguely: "The weather?"

"Yes. Looks a bit like rain. Hadn't

you noticed?" said Mrs. Hedges, rather pityingly.

"Oh, yes, the sun's gone in," murmured Caroline, rousing herself.

"Are you sure you'll be all right on your own?" asked Mrs. Hedges.

"Yes, thank you," Caroline answered, with a faint smile to prove it. "I'll cook myself something in a minute."

But she sat on at the desk after the daily had given her a last interested and sympathetic look and ridden off on her bicycle, eager to talk the whole thing over with her elderly husband, who would not be greatly concerned so long as it didn't mean her losing her job, but who would have to listen, whatever he thought.

Caroline was pondering over Gordon's extraordinary way of life. What risks he had taken in making his second home with her, his bigamously married wife, not forty miles from Fulhaven, a popular resort, where he lived intermittently with his official one. Somebody from Oxridge who knew him might easily have seen him at Fulhaven; when he was supposed to be elsewhere. How would he have carried that off? Surely he couldn't have continued that sort of double existence for long without some crisis arising. Perhaps Neil was right, and he had not meant it to last long.

She gave a little shiver, remembering that torn out address of the lonely holiday cottage. Then she blinked and uttered an exclamation aloud. She had seen a figure moving furtively but very swiftly into the shelter of the willows. She had caught the sudden movement only briefly, as she glanced up, but she was certain of what she had glimpsed.

She stood and leaned over the desk, trying to get a wider view, for it had seemed to her that the figure had moved just out of her range of vision. A few drops of rain bespattered the window panes as she looked, but she took no heed of them. The figure remained out of sight.

Her alarm changed to a wry amusement

as she thought of what must be the explanation. Of course it was the motor-cyclist, or a colleague, back on the job. If it was Gordon who had engaged them — and no doubt it was — then they would not know that their employer was dead, that husband and wife were already parted by something more drastic than divorce.

"I'm very much afraid that you're not going to get paid, my man," she murmured to the now invisible watcher.

She imagined the detective agency sending in information and bills marked 'Private', and addressed to Gordon. She wondered whether she would be justified in opening them and reading the contents or whether she ought to send them back unopened with 'Moved away' or 'Address unknown', written on the envelopes. She decided that curiosity would compel her to open them.

From the kitchen sounded the yowl of a cat. There was a note of fear in it.

A dog in the garden probably, thought Caroline, and Colonel had seen it from the window. But in that case, there should be anger and defiance in the cry. Perhaps she had imagined the fear. Or he might simply want to go out in a hurry for purposes of nature. She had better go and see. It was time she got herself a meal, in any case. She was not hungry, but she must eat. 'To keep her strength up,' Mrs. Hedges would say.

The kitchen door was open, and she went in, saying: "Where are you, Colonel? What's the matter?"

Then she saw the cat on the window-ledge, eyes fixed in a hostile glare, back arched and fur on end. But the glare was directed, not into the garden, but towards her. In the instant that she realized that it was actually directed at something behind her, she whirled round galvanized by terror. The blow that had been intended for her head hit her shoulder and the weapon slipped from unnerved fingers and fell with a clatter to the floor. Instinctively, she kicked it under the table and screamed and screamed, clutching her shoulder, till the man who had dropped the gun in a momentary weakness recalled his desperate resolution and seized her by the throat.

16

WHEN her own voice failed her, Caroline thought she could hear, through the roaring in her ears, another voice taking up the screaming, and after darkness and silence had descended, in a temporary flicker of consciousness had a brief vision of Mrs. Hedges, staring down at her with bulging eyes while clasping an armful of towels, teacloths and underwear to her mackintoshed bosom. So, when she finally woke from what seemed to have been a night disturbed by pain and nightmare, the first thing she croaked was the name of her help.

"Thank God!" said a man's voice fervently, and Neil's face swam into view, his fiery hair rumpled, his tawny eyes full of worry and anger. "But don't try to talk, darling." And now the eyes seemed to be trying to convey a warning.

She didn't really want to talk, so instead she merely mouthed: "Mrs. Hedges?"

Neil nodded understandingly. "She came back because of the rain, bless her!" he said. "She was afraid you wouldn't notice and she was concerned about the washing. She probably saved your life."

"Feeling a little better, Mrs. Lane?" said a quiet man, appearing by her side, and taking her wrist from under the blanket that covered her.

Looking over his shoulder was a man in dark blue uniform with shining buttons.

"I shall want a statement from her as soon as she can give it, Doctor," he said.

"Which won't be yet awhile," replied the doctor, whom she now recognized as the local police surgeon, who had a general practice in Oxridge.

"I should think not," said Neil. "In

any case, I've already told you why she was attacked."

But Caroline herself had not yet grasped the reason. She wanted to say so, but the thought brought back the horror of the moment when she had seen Dobson, with a rose in his lapel and murder in his eyes, coming at her from behind her own kitchen door, ready to club her with the butt of the revolver in his hand. She closed her eyes and shivered.

"That's enough. You're upsetting her," murmured the doctor.

"Well, as I said, it was the photograph in the paper that did it." Neil was saying, his voice coming from a little distance now, but sounding as if he was enunciating rather carefully.

She realized he intended her to hear this, so she tried to concentrate and listen, while keeping her eyes shut.

"Dobson evidently saw it, and was afraid Mrs. Lane would see it, too, and recognize it as her husband's portrait and go to the police. That would have provided the link between him and Lane, whereas there was nothing at all to connect him with Lessing."

"Lessing, The Fulhaven Victim?" said the doctor, turning away, curiosity evidently getting the better of him.

"That's right. Lessing was also Lane. That's what Dobson was afraid of the police finding out. But he was too late. Mrs. Lane *had* seen the picture, and she had phoned me to tell me about it. That's why I came down to see her." Naturally she was very disturbed and upset at the likeness to her husband, and wanted my advice on what she should do."

Caroline heard the two-toned siren of an ambulance approaching and heard the doctor mutter: "And about time!"

She knew, however, that the timing was perfect. The delay — if there had really been one — had enabled her to get Neil's message. He was going to tell the police everything, *except* that she had known all along that it was her husband who had been found dead in the Fulhaven shelter and that she had been the first to discover him there.

For several days she lay in hospital with a bruised throat and a fractured collar-bone and all the symptoms of severe shock. She had visitors, of course. One was Chief Inspector Smith, and one was a little grey-haired woman with eyes like Neil's who kissed her and called her a poor darling.

Then the time came when she was sitting up in bed, almost restored to her normal self, and Neil came striding in, with a bunch of bronze chrysanthemums held awkwardly in his arms. The eyes that so nearly matched them in colour brightened when he saw her.

"You're better." he said in pleased tones, dropping the flowers on the counterpane.

She smiled and nodded, gathering up the chrysanthemums and sniffing their odd, pungent scent with delight.

"Did you know, your mother came

to see me," she told him.

"Yes. I couldn't hold her back once she knew about you. My father, too, is waiting for the chance to make a fuss of you," he said, grinning.

"I don't deserve it," declared Caroline ruefully. "I've been a shocking coward."

"That's not what they think," said Neil.

"I should have gone to the police straight away, that Friday night," said Caroline, shaking her head.

"You didn't tell them about — " began Neil, in a lowered voice, glancing quickly round the small private room as if fearful of listeners.

"No," said Caroline. "I stuck to our previous story. But I said I went to Fulhaven because I had become suspicious of Gordon and put up at Regency House because I found the address among his things. But Mr. Smith didn't seem all that interested in what *I'd* done. It was Gordon's connection with Dobson he wanted to know about. He told me Dobson was dead." She looked at Neil rather anxiously.

"Yes," he said. "He came bursting out of your front door, looking like a maniac, just as I was getting out of my car. His nerve seemed to have completely gone. I could hear your Mrs. Hedges screaming like a banshee, only I didn't know it was her, of course. I shouted at Dobson to stop, but he just went on running towards his own car. Then he seemed to falter and stagger, made a queer snorting noise and dropped. He was dead by the time the ambulance came. A fatal coronary, apparently. I suppose he'd been living under a fearful strain since Friday, and he wasn't so young. You were right about him, Caroline. I wish I hadn't been so bloody clever in pulling down all the evidence you built up against him."

She never heard him swear before or heard such bitterness in his tone.

"Don't blame yourself," she said. "You had to say what you thought."

He shook his head. "If it hadn't been

for Mrs. Hedges — "

"And Colonel," Caroline told him, smiling. "It was he who really warned me in time. Otherwise I might have a cracked skull instead of just a collarbone."

"We'll apply for that medal they give life-saving animals," said Neil, looking more cheerful.

"He'd rather have a good tuck-in, I think," said Caroline. "And what about a reward for Mrs. Hedges?"

"She's had all she wants," said Neil grinning again. "A highly dramatic role in an affair that has been hitting the headlines in the newspapers — her favourite one, anyway, and her own portrait on the front page."

"I can't think why Dobson didn't shoot me, instead of trying to club me with that revolver," mused Caroline.

"I think he knew enough about firearms to be afraid of the police discovering it was the same weapon that had killed Lessing in Fulhaven," said Neil. "That was the thing he was trying at all costs to avoid, any link up with that case."

"I don't think he was naturally a killer," murmured Caroline. "In fact, I'm sure he wasn't, by the way he went to pieces in the end. I can almost feel sorry for him. You know, it was he who hired the motor-cyclist, don't you? It was a man from that detective agency I mentioned."

"Yes, you were right about that, too," said Neil. "You were right about everything."

"Except about Dobson's motive," Caroline said. "Mr. Smith hinted that he'd got some information from the secretary at that place — who must listen at doors. I think — and he seems to think that Dobson knew Gordon, when he was Longton, better than you think, that they were both engaged in some racket, smuggling stuff out of the country for cash, and that Gordon disappeared with the takings."

"Then I suppose you must have given the man the hope of getting some of the money back, when you came to him with your enquiry and your tell-tale photograph of your missing husband," said Neil.

"And perhaps he thought I'd had a phone-call from Gordon telling me to meet him in Fulhaven, when his spy told him I'd gone there," said Caroline. "Maybe he took the gun mainly to intimidate Gordon. I wonder what happened, if there was a tussle and the gun went off, or if Gordon goaded him beyond endurance."

"I don't suppose we shall ever know," murmured Neil, "And it's all over now, Caroline." He laid his hand on hers and kept it there.

With her face buried in the chrysan-themums, now held cradled in her one good arm, Caroline said suddenly:

"Were you at a party when you telephoned that Sunday night, Neil?"

An odd, wary expression came over his face, then he grinned. "No," he said. "I was just with some friends. We were rehearsing."

"Rehearsing?" she repeated, astonished.

"I play the cello in an amateur string-quarter," he confessed, actually blushing slightly. "We hope one day we might even be able to turn professional. Do you mind?"

"Mind?" said Caroline. "I think it's marvellous. I'd love to hear you. Why on earth should I mind?"

He gave her a very straight look. "My wife minded," he said. "That was one of the reasons we broke up. That's why I was afraid to tell you before."

"I see," murmured Caroline, making no pretence of not understanding.

Pressing the hand he held, but only gently, he said: "You won't have to have that make-believe divorce now. You're a widow.

"In a way," said Caroline. "By law, I was never actually a wife, I suppose."

He gave her an extraordinarily tender smile.

"Never mind," he said. "When you're ready to become the genuine article, my darling, just let me know."

A FOOT IN THE GRAVE
Bruce Marshall

About to be imprisoned and tortured in Buenos Aires, John Smith escapes, only to become involved in an aeroplane hijacking.

DEAD TROUBLE
Martin Carroll

Trespassing brought Jennifer Denning more than she bargained for. She was totally unprepared for the violence which was to lie in her path.

HOURS TO KILL
Ursula Curtiss

Margaret went to New Mexico to look after her sick sister's rented house and felt a sharp edge of fear when the absent landlady arrived.

THE DEATH OF ABBE DIDIER
Richard Grayson

Inspector Gautier of the Sûreté investigates three crimes which are strangely connected.

NIGHTMARE TIME
Hugh Pentecost

Have the missing major and his wife met with foul play somewhere in the Beaumont Hotel, or is their disappearance a carefully planned step in an act of treason?

BLOOD WILL OUT
Margaret Carr

Why was the manor house so oddly familiar to Elinor Howard? Who would have guessed that a Sunday School outing could lead to murder?

THE DRACULA MURDERS
Philip Daniels

The Horror Ball was interrupted by a spectral figure who warned the merrymakers they were tampering with the unknown.

THE LADIES
OF LAMBTON GREEN
Liza Shepherd

Why did murdered Robin Colquhoun's picture pose such a threat to the ladies of Lambton Green?

CARNABY
AND THE GAOLBREAKERS
Peter N. Walker

Detective Sergeant James Aloysius Carnaby-King is sent to prison as bait. When he joins in an escape he is thrown headfirst into a vicious murder hunt.

MUD IN HIS EYE
Gerald Hammond

The harbourmaster's body is found mangled beneath Major Smyle's yacht. What is the sinister significance of the illicit oysters?

THE SCAVENGERS
Bill Knox

Among the masses of struggling fish in the *Tecta*'s nets was a larger, darker, ominously motionless form . . . the body of a skin diver.

DEATH IN ARCADY
Stella Phillips

Detective Inspector Matthew Furnival works unofficially with the local police when a brutal murder takes place in a caravan camp.

STORM CENTRE
Douglas Clark

Detective Chief Superintendent Masters, temporarily lecturing in a police staff college, finds there's more to the job than a few weeks relaxation in a rural setting.

THE MANUSCRIPT MURDERS
Roy Harley Lewis

Antiquarian bookseller Matthew Coll, acquires a rare 16th century manuscript. But when the Dutch professor who had discovered the journal is murdered, Coll begins to doubt its authenticity.

SHARENDEL
Margaret Carr

Ruth didn't want all that money. And she didn't want Aunt Cass to die. But at Sharendel things looked different. She began to wonder if she had a split personality.

MURDER TO BURN
Laurie Mantell

Sergeants Steven Arrow and Lance Brendon, of the New Zealand police force, come upon a woman's body in the water. When the dead woman is identified they begin to realise that they are investigating a complex fraud.

YOU CAN HELP ME
Maisie Birmingham

Whilst running the Citizens' Advice Bureau, Kate Weatherley is attacked with no apparent motive. Then the body of one of her clients is found in her room.

DAGGERS DRAWN
Margaret Carr

Stacey Manston was the kind of girl who could take most things in her stride, but three murders were something different . . .

THE MONTMARTRE MURDERS
Richard Grayson

Inspector Gautier of Sûreté investigates the disappearance of artist Théo, the heir to a fortune.

GRIZZLY TRAIL
Gwen Moffat

Miss Pink, alone in the Rockies, helps in a search for missing hikers, solves two cruel murders and has the most terrifying experience of her life when she meets a grizzly bear!

BLINDMAN'S BLUFF
Margaret Carr

Kate Deverill had considered suicide. It was one way out — and preferable to being murdered.